"Maybe it's just lu̲... want to find out..."

"You mean, about how it would be..." As if she hadn't thought about it nonstop the whole time she'd spent at this place. How it would be if they were married, if this was their ranch, if Sarah was their child... The longing that filled her heart threatened to bring tears to her eyes.

He held her firmly in his grasp. "I need you. We all need you. But do you need us?"

She nodded. Afraid to let him know just how much she needed, wanted, loved this place, this family, this man. The words were waiting to be said. But not now. Maybe never. Not until she was sure of him.

Dear Reader,

Take one married mom, add a surprise night of passion with her almost ex-husband, and what do you get? *Welcome Home, Daddy!* In Kristin Morgan's wonderful Romance, Rachel and Ross Murdock are now blessed with a baby on the way—and a second chance at marriage. That means Ross has only nine months to show his wife he's a FABULOUS FATHER!

Now take an any-minute-mom-to-be whose baby decides to make an appearance while she's snowbound at her handsome boss's cabin. What do you get? *An Unexpected Delivery* by Laurie Paige—a BUNDLES OF JOY book that will bring a big smile.

When one of THE BAKER BROOD hires a sexy detective to find her missing brother, she never expects to find herself walking down the aisle in Carla Cassidy's *An Impromptu Proposal*.

What's a single daddy to do when he falls for a woman with no memory? What if she's another man's wife—or another child's mother? Find out in Carol Grace's *The Rancher and the Lost Bride*.

Lynn Bulock's *And Mommy Makes Three* tells the tale of a little boy who wants a mom—and finds one in the "Story Lady" at the local library. Problem is, Dad isn't looking for a new Mrs.!

In Elizabeth Krueger's *Family Mine*, a very eligible bachelor returns to town, prepared to make an honest woman out of a single mother—but she has other ideas for him....

Finally, take six irresistible, emotional love stories by six terrific authors—and what do you get? Silhouette Romance— every month!

Enjoy every last one,

Melissa Senate
Senior Editor

Please address questions and book requests to:
Silhouette Reader Service
U.S.: 3010 Walden Ave., P.O. Box 1325, Buffalo, NY 14269
Canadian: P.O. Box 609, Fort Erie, Ont. L2A 5X3

THE RANCHER AND THE LOST BRIDE

Carol Grace

Silhouette

ROMANCE™

Published by Silhouette Books

America's Publisher of Contemporary Romance

For my little niece, Emily Noel, born in China,
September 1993, now residing in Alaska.
Welcome to the family!
Love, Aunt Carol Grace

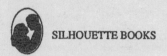 SILHOUETTE BOOKS

ISBN 0-373-19153-7

THE RANCHER AND THE LOST BRIDE

Books by Carol Grace

Silhouette Romance

*Miramar Inn

CAROL GRACE

has always been interested in travel and living abroad. She spent her junior year in college in France and toured the world working on the hospital ship *HOPE*. She and her husband spent the first year and a half of their marriage in Iran, where they both taught English. Then, with their toddler daughter, they lived in Algeria for two years.

Carol says that writing is another way of making her life exciting. Her office is an Airstream trailer parked behind her mountaintop home, which overlooks the Pacific Ocean and which she shares with her inventor husband, their daughter, who is now sixteen years old, and their eleven-year-old son.

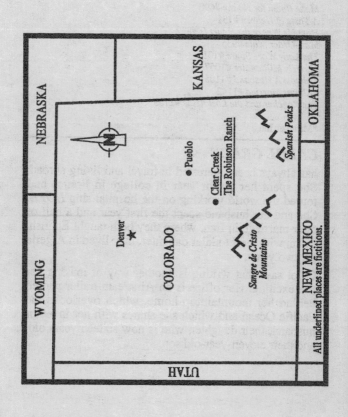

All underlined places are fictitious.

Chapter One

The sun sank behind the seven-thousand-foot-high Spanish Peaks as the woman pounded the last stake into the ground to anchor her small tent to the dry earth. She was all alone in the vast valley, bordered by the Sangre de Cristos on one side and the Peaks on the other. There were no other campers and that was fine with her. Loneliness was something she'd have to get used to. She might as well start now.

In fact, she'd come to this remote camping area to get away from people, from prying eyes, from pitying glances, to find peace. To find herself. To find out who she was and what would become of her now that the future she had planned was not to be. Somber gray clouds skittered across the darkening sky. The threat of a storm didn't frighten her. Nothing frightened her anymore. The worst had already happened. A cold wind blew through the valley and the woman thrust her arms into the sleeves of a hooded sweatshirt, and built a small campfire.

Her solitary meal was soup made from a freeze-dried mix augmented with a handful of fresh mushrooms and a dash of herbs. She sipped her soup thinking that everything tasted better when eaten outside. Maybe her appetite was returning to her at last. If so, maybe her interest in the future would soon follow. Right now all she could think of was what had happened. After dinner she fished a bottle of dry white wine from the bottom of her backpack and poured some into a tin cup. Cross-legged, she sat on the ground drinking her wine and gazing into the flames as she fought a losing battle with her memories. She'd come all this way and yet they followed her still. The stillness of an empty church. Unopened presents. A wedding that never took place, a dream that never came true and never would come true. Not now. Not ever.

She glanced at the blue-black clouds above and extinguished the fire with water from a nearby stream, then quickly retired to the shelter of her snug little tent and the warmth of her down sleeping bag. But the ground was hard, even with the foam sleeping pad under her.

Restless, she reached into her pocket, took out a necklace and ran her fingers over the gold and diamonds on one side and the engraved message on the other. She should never have brought it with her, an expensive pendant like that. Why did she want it anyway, as a tangible reminder of her loss? Maybe she needed to be reminded that while diamonds are forever, love isn't.

Thunder rumbled loudly in the distance and she shivered with apprehension. She finally drifted off into an uneasy sleep, still clutching the necklace in her hand. Sometime around midnight she was jarred awake by rain drumming on the blue nylon above her and the wind howling around her tent, threatening to blow it over. Lightning forked across the sky and thunder rolled again, closer and louder.

A tremor of fear shook her. She sat up and gripped the aluminum pole that supported the tent. Suddenly a brilliant light went off in her face like a blinding flashbulb. A shaft of pain knifed through her body. An unearthly force catapulted her into the air and dropped her on the ground like a shapeless rag doll.

"Oh, my God!" she screamed, and then everything went black.

Parker Robinson stood on his front porch and inhaled the fragrant fresh air that always followed a storm. Despite the hectic nature of lambing season, the ongoing dispute with his father over which breed of sheep to raise and his twelve-year-old daughter's dislike of her boarding school, life was pretty good. Taking a minute to survey the vast expanse of the Robinson Ranch, he liked what he saw. And most of what he saw was all his. His and his father's. A fertile green valley ringed with purple mountains and no people to clutter the landscape or mar the silence, except the ones who either worked for him or were related to him.

Just as he was enjoying that same silence, his sheepdogs, the ones who could herd all day without making a sound, came racing toward him barking their heads off. He held out his hands palms forward, signaling them to calm down. But they raced back and forth in the driveway until he finally decided they must be trying to tell him something. He turned and almost ran into his father at the front door.

"What's going on?" the old man asked, pushing his shaggy gray hair from his forehead with one gnarled hand.

"Don't know," Parker said. "Maybe a ewe in trouble, maybe a lamb caught in a fence. I'll go see." He brushed past his father to get his black bag that had the shears, the towels, a blanket, a lubricant and disinfectant.

"Want some help?" his father asked as Parker came back through the living room.

Parker shook his head. "I'll take the truck and see what's happening. Chances are it's nothing more than a gopher they're after, but it could be a coyote worrying the sheep. If you have time could you check the lambing pens for me? I've got yearlings in labor who don't know what they're doing."

His father nodded. Parker got into the truck and followed the dogs as they ran ahead of him. Crisscrossing the lush green fields of clover and alfalfa, they continued to bark and look over their shoulders to make sure he was still there. "This better not be a wild-goose chase," he muttered. "I haven't got time for a joyride today."

When the dogs finally stopped and circled an object on the ground the approximate size of a three-year-old sheep, Parker stopped his truck, grabbed his black bag and jumped out. This time the dogs were making soft growling sounds deep in their throats as they did when they found a lost or a lame sheep.

But this was not a sheep. This curled-up creature with the matted brown hair, tattered clothes and mud-splattered skin was human. Parker knelt on the ground beside the prostrate figure and felt for a pulse. Faint but erratic. He loosened the tattered shirt and drew a sudden sharp breath at the sight of her pale breasts, half-hidden by scraps of a silk bra. Not only human, but a woman. A woman who was trembling with cold and shock. What the hell was she doing here, only half-alive in the middle of his pasture?

But this was no time for questions. If this were a newborn lamb he'd rub it dry, wrap it in a bedding and put it under a heat lamp. But a woman? He didn't know what to do with a woman. He never had. He yanked the blanket out of his bag and as carefully as if she were a lamb, wrapped her in it. With two strong arms, Parker lifted the woman, cradled her with her face against his chest, and carried her to the truck.

Half seated, half lying on the front seat next to him with the blanket around her, her eyelids fluttered wildly and her lips were dry and parched. But it was her hair that startled him, lying in stiff clumps of brown and singed at the ends. As he drove fast and frantically back to the house, the dogs following in his wake, he wondered if she'd been thrown from a horse or had a heart attack. Then he thought of the storm, of the thunder and lightning, and he wondered if she'd been struck.

Brakes squealing, he pulled the truck up to the front steps of the ranch house, lifted the woman still wrapped in the blanket and carried her up the front steps. She weighed more than a newborn lamb, but something less than a shearling. Without the bulk. This woman was slender and fine-boned. And sick, very sick.

"What is it?" his father called as he came limping around the corner of the barn.

"Not sure. Some kind of injury. Call Doc Haller, would you?" Parker tossed the words over his shoulder. "Ask him to come out right away?"

"You mean Doc Stevens, don't ya? What's wrong with it?" Emilio Robinson asked with a frown.

"It's not an *it*, it's a woman." Parker was breathing hard. Either he was badly out of shape or badly worried. He should be worried. He had a sick woman on his hands, or in his arms, to be precise. A woman who'd been hurt or injured on his property.

Parker shifted the woman in his arms, holding her tightly, feeling her body tremble. His father, as if propelled by the urgency in Parker's voice, caught up with his son at the front door and held it open. "What did you say?"

"A woman," Parker said tersely. "Call the doc. Tell him it's urgent."

His father nodded and went to the telephone in the kitchen as fast as his uneven gait would let him.

Parker's brain raced. What to do? Where to put her? If this was a newborn lamb he'd found, stiff and cold and unconscious, he'd dip the lamb into water as hot as his elbow could stand, to warm it up. Then he'd rub it dry with coarse cloth and get it some warm milk. Put it under a heat lamp and keep it under observation.

He carried her into the bathroom next to the den and awkwardly bent over the tub and turned on both faucets for the right mixture. Then he sat on the commode with her still in his arms and let the steam surround them. It seemed to him that she wasn't shaking quite so much. His father knocked on the door and stuck his head in.

"He's comin' as quick as he can. But he's got some other emergency he's gotta see to first. Said to tell you he doesn't normally make house calls, but seein' it's you, he knows you don't bother him 'less it's really something . . . And keep her warm, case she's in shock, he says."

"Right," Parker agreed, frowning at the woman lying stiffly in his arms, noticing her high cheekbones, a straight, aristocratic nose, a firm chin. Smudged and dirty and cold.

"Looks bad, don't she?" his father noted in his raspy voice. "What happened?"

Parker shook his head. "No idea. Reminds me of a newborn. Only thing I know to do is treat her like one." He looked up at his father's lined face. "You have any ideas?"

"Only what you're doin'. Nobody as good as you when it comes to a sick sheep."

"Never have been any good with women, though," Parker muttered, and he reached over to turn the water off.

"I'll get the blankets," his father offered. "Put her in the den?" He closed the door behind him without waiting for an answer.

Parker opened his mouth to tell him not to leave him alone with this woman, but it was too late. He didn't want to take what remained of her clothes off and put her in the large, old-fashioned tub. But he couldn't wait for the doctor. He had to do something. His father was right. He'd nursed many a lamb through critical times, ones others had given up on. Brought them back to life. But that didn't mean he knew what to do now. When his daughter was small they'd had a housekeeper. She'd taken care of Sarah sick or well. Then she left and Sarah had gone away to school.

He was stalling. And he had an emergency on his hands. Thinking of the past only put off what had to be done. Now. He peeled her shirt off her body. It was ripped, torn and frayed at the edges. Her jeans were damp. He tugged, inching them off her legs, and left them in a heap on the floor. Next, panties and bra. He could leave them on her. But they were damp, too, molded to her body. He took a deep breath and took them off, his calloused fingers brushing against her cool, soft skin. There was an ugly purple bruise on one hip. A cut on her shin. Aside from that, she had a lovely body, long legs, slim hips and beautiful full breasts.

Her eyelids fluttered open and just before he put her into the water she gave him a long reproachful look with huge gray-blue eyes and he almost dropped her.

"Sorry," he muttered. "I'm doing this for your own good."

She buried her face in his shirt as if she couldn't stand to look at him. He didn't blame her. What would it be like to wake up in a strange place, staring up into a stranger's face knowing he'd just undressed you? But she didn't know, did she? And he'd never tell. He lowered her into the bath, trying not to look at her long legs, her rounded breasts, pale stomach, except in a clinical way, the way he might examine an injured lamb. But this was no lamb. This was a woman. Oh, God, what had he gotten himself into?

She sank so low into the water he was afraid she'd drown. He knelt on the bathmat next to the tub to catch her, but she floated to the surface, her hair spread out in clumps around her face, the rosy tips of her breasts breaking the surface. He wrenched his gaze away to look into her eyes, little slits of slate gray that watched him warily.

"Can you talk?" he asked, rocking back on his haunches.

After a long silence, she shook her head very slightly. Then she squeezed her eyes shut in pain and slid farther into the water. What if she drowned? Where was the doctor?

"Where does it hurt?" he asked, leaning forward.

No answer.

He clamped his mouth shut. He didn't know what he was doing, playing sheep doctor with a woman. What if she passed out again? Or had a heart attack? Desperate, he took a washcloth from the shelf, soaked it in warm water, and ran it over her forehead, wiping the dirt away and uncovering a long, shallow laceration. She winced and opened her eyes to give him an accusing look.

"I'm sorry," he said again. He was tired of being sorry. He kept his eyes on her face. "The doctor's on his way." He'd better be on his way. "In the meantime I'm trying to help." She may not believe that, he thought, but he didn't know what else to do. What he'd like to do was get rid of her, get out of here and get back to grafting orphan lambs, mending fences, feeding sheep, checking on the ranch hands, hiring a new cook, in short, running a six-hundred-acre sheep ranch.

As if she'd read his thoughts, her lips moved. "Sorry," she said. Or did he just imagine it?

He shrugged. "Don't worry about it," he said. That's right. That's reassuring. She's lying naked in some strange tub with some strange guy looking down at her and he tells her not to worry. Well, anyway, she ought to be warm by now. "Let's get you out of there," he said gruffly.

She raised her arms. So she heard. She understood. But did she trust him? She must, because she wrapped her arms around him and he lifted her out of the tub, wrapped a huge bath towel around her and carried her into the den where his father had opened the daybed and put fresh sheets on it. He'd even laid out a pair of men's flannel pajamas, still in their Christmas box, a gift from some distant relative. Did his father expect him to dress her, too?

Parker gritted his teeth, put the woman on the bed, patted her dry with the towel, and quickly, awkwardly, pulled the pants up over her hips and as gently as possible stuffed her arms into the sleeves and conveniently forgot about the buttons. His fingers were shaking too much to try any buttons. It had been a long time since he'd dressed or undressed a woman, and they'd been more cooperative as he remembered, but never more beautiful, even with the abrasions and bruises. He covered her with a striped sheet and two wool blankets and stood at the side of the bed breathing heavily, his arms crossed over his chest. The sight of her bruises and cuts worried him. Should he use some disinfectant on them? The thought of possible internal injuries kept his stomach in knots. Should he have moved her at all or left her in the field? Was she asleep now or awake, conscious or unconscious? Where the hell was that medic?

She was conscious. Barely. Enough to know she had a headache. And that every muscle in her body screamed out in pain. Muscles she didn't know about. What else didn't she know about? She didn't know where she was or who he was, this tall man who towered over her, staring down at her with deep blue penetrating eyes. And what was worse, she didn't have any idea who *she* was or what she was doing there. A moan escaped her lips and the room spun around. But the man didn't move. He was the only constant in her small universe. What had he said? Something about a doctor. Maybe she had the flu. That's what it felt like. Like the worst Type B flu she could imagine. She wanted to ask if that's what it was.

But she couldn't speak. Her throat was too tight, her lips dry. The lines in the man's rugged face told her he was worried. About her? She closed her eyes and drifted into unconsciousness, thinking about the man, wishing she could say something to erase those worry lines. To tell him everything was going to be okay.

When the doctor finally came he held an instrument to her chest and she gasped at the shock of cold metal against her skin that jerked her back to consciousness.

"Aha, little lady," he said. "So you've decided to join us."

He smelled like antiseptic and soap and felt starchy, not like the man with the blue eyes whose flannel shirt was soft and comforting and who smelled like worn leather and pipe tobacco and the outdoors. When she opened her eyes she saw an old man at the door, either on his way in or out, but the other man was still there, blue eyes, exactly where he'd been, at the side of her bed while the doctor sat on the other side poking and prodding and asking questions like, "Does it hurt there? There? How about there?"

She wanted to scream that it hurt all over. She wanted to tell them all to go away and leave her alone, to stop staring, asking, probing.

But they didn't. They asked harder questions, like "Who are you? Where did you come from? What are you doing here?"

She shook her head very slightly. Maybe if she didn't jar her brain it would all come back to her. Her name, her address, her reason for being there. But where was there? If she could speak she'd like to ask them a few questions of her own. "Who are *you?*" and "Where *am* I?" But they acted like she wasn't even there, the three of them discussing what to do with her as if she were a sack of cement. Or in a coma. Instead of just having a bad case of flu.

"Like to put her in the hospital, run some tests," the doctor said, pulling out a disposable needle. Expertly he leaned over and inserted it into her upper arm. It stung. She gasped and he apologized. A little late for that, she thought, closing her eyes to block out the pain.

"But it's a long ride just to the highway on a dirt road," he continued, "so for the moment the best thing is to leave her where she is."

"What?" Surprise, shock and dismay all crowded into that one word.

Even with her eyes closed, she knew it was the blue-eyed, tall man who'd said it. The deep voice matched the eyes, the large hands, the broad shoulders.

"But, Doc, I've got my hands full. Lambing season. I'm short on help. We can't possibly..."

"Leave her, we'll manage." It was an old voice, tinged with an accent. It was the old man in the door with the sorrowful dark eyes.

"For how long?" the young man asked, barely able to contain his irritation.

She felt the mattress shift. The doctor rose from her bedside. "Can't say, Parker. Don't know what's wrong with her. Or rather, I know what's wrong, irregular heartbeat, burns, bruises, lacerations, low blood pressure. I just don't know what caused it. You found her out in the field. Anything else in sight? Horse? Tent? No idea what she was doing there?''

"I wasn't looking,'' the man said. Parker. That was his name. Parker. "I'll have to go back. She couldn't have just dropped there, fallen from outer space.''

"Maybe her spaceship's coming back to get her later.'' The doctor chuckled.

Her mind spun in circles. Maybe it wasn't a joke. Maybe she *was* an alien. She certainly felt like one. An alien with the flu.

"In the meantime she needs plenty of fluids, soft food, lots of rest. I know it sounds like a full-time job, but what can I say? What can I do with her? You found her. I'm afraid you've got her, temporarily at least.''

There was silence in the room except for the clink of medical instruments, a bag being zipped shut. Not a happy silence. The hush that follows an unwelcome pronouncement. A resigned silence. Then footsteps. And she was alone. Without opening her eyes she knew it, felt it, sensed it. And the questions they'd asked reverberated in the room. Who, where, why? The last thing she remembered were the voices in the hall, half spoken, half whispered.

"Not possible.''

"But what else . . .''

"I don't care.''

"Only a few days and maybe . . .''

"Worst possible time.''

The next time she woke up it was dark outside the window. A lamp on a tall oak dresser cast a pool of light across the room, illuminating the tall cowboy slouched in a chair opposite her bed. The one who didn't want her there at this worst possible time, who had his hands full without her. She thought of slipping away in the night, perhaps right now. He wouldn't mind. He might even help her leave. She lifted the edge of the blanket.

"Hey. What're you doing?" He got up out of his chair, unwinding his lanky body to walk to her bed, and reached for a glass on the nightstand. He didn't wait for her to answer his question before he asked another. "Thirsty?"

She shook her head. Her mouth was parched but she wouldn't take anything from him. Nothing. She was leaving as soon as she could. But before she could swing her legs over the side of the mattress, he sat on the edge of the bed and put one strong arm around her to hoist her up against the headboard. Then he held the glass to her lips and unwillingly she took one tentative sip of the cool water then gulped it so thirstily she could have sworn he rolled his eyes heavenward at her stubborn obstinacy. Or was it just what she thought he *would* do. Water dribbled down her chin. He set the glass down and mopped her chin, throat and chest with a tissue. She felt her face burn, as well as the trail he made with his fingers. It was not from fever, it was embarrassment. Had she always been a klutz or was it the sickness?

If she could talk she'd apologize. But the next thing she knew he was spooning yogurt from a carton into her mouth, so soothing to her sore throat it brought tears to her eyes. Or maybe it was being treated like a baby that brought the tears. It was humiliating. Especially knowing how much he didn't want her there. How much he resented her presence. She didn't remember much, but she remembered that. She turned her face toward the window, but he placed his thumb under her chin and firmly turned it back toward him. "Eat," he said. "Doctor's orders." And he pushed another

spoonful into her mouth. And another. It suddenly
dawned on her she was in the care of a tyrant. A stern-
faced, weather-beaten tyrant. The best-looking tyrant
she'd ever seen.

When she'd finished the entire container he propped
a pillow under her head and stood. "Anything else?"
he asked brusquely, forgetting she couldn't speak. "Oh,
yes, the bathroom."

She shook her head violently, pushed the blankets off
the bed and attempted to stand. If she had to crawl on
all fours she'd get to the bathroom by herself, even if it
was half a mile away. But she never got a chance to try.
Before her feet hit the ground he'd picked her up again,
like a sack of potatoes this time, and headed out the
door and down the hall a few steps.

She took a deep breath and tried to pound on his
back with her fists, but she couldn't make a fist. She
had no strength in her hands. Or anywhere.
"Put...me...down," she said. The voice that said those
words couldn't be hers. It sounded weak and pitiful.
But it startled him so much he put her down at the
bathroom door, supporting her by cupping her elbows
in his hands.

"I didn't know you could talk," he said, his face cast
in shadows from the overhead hall light fixture.

"I didn't know I could, either," she admitted in a half
whisper. The truth was she had nothing to say. What
was the point of talking if you had no name, no past
and no future? "I'll just..." She looked at the bathroom door.

"Do you want me to..."

"No!" With a burst of energy she pushed the door
open and closed it firmly behind her. She braced her
arms on the washstand where she stood still and took

several deep breaths. Her head pounded and her legs felt like jelly. Dimly she noted a new toothbrush, hand lotion and a stack of clean towels. What was this, a hotel? A guest ranch? A sanitarium for people who'd lost their minds? Along the wall was a huge claw-foot porcelain tub with a damp bath mat hung over the side.

She drew her eyebrows together and tried to remember. The hot water, the gentle hands that washed her brow, the strong arms that lifted her in and out. Whose? His? When she'd finished doing what she'd come to do, she took a brief glance at the mirror and gasped in horror. The creature that looked back at her was a witch, a woman from a horror movie, her hair standing on end, one eye blackened, an ugly cut across her forehead. She shuddered and opened the door. He was still there, leaning against the wall, waiting for her. He had a way of standing, or sitting, or just looking that betrayed none of the impatience he must feel. None of the resentment she *knew* he felt. As if he had nothing better to do than wait outside the bathroom. Instead of chastising her for taking so long, he only said, "Ready?" and picked her up without waiting for an answer and put her back in bed.

Chapter Two

One week and forty newborn lambs later, all of them healthy and dropped on range pasture, Parker stood on his front porch again, this time watching the latest in the line of cooks disappear over the horizon in his pickup truck. Four of his men rode up on horseback and asked what happened this time.

Parker ran his hand through his hair. "Damned if I know. I paid that cook twice what he was worth."

"I thought he was all right," Randy said, reaching down to calm his horse.

"Hey, Parker, what next? The agency gonna send somebody else?"

"Tomorrow. Tonight we're on our own. There oughta be some leftovers."

A third man, the one they called Lefty, frowned. "A man can't live on leftovers," he protested.

"For one night?" Parker asked. He knew they looked forward to a hearty meal after a hard day on the range, but what was he supposed to do, conjure up a cook out of nowhere? They were hard to come by and the good ones wanted to be closer to town.

After a few more or less amiable requests for Parker to get a new cook *now,* the men rode off. This was the most critical time on a sheep ranch and here was Parker, stuck with a sick woman, without a memory, in his den and no cook in his kitchen.

To top it off his daughter would be home on Friday for the weekend. A twelve-year-old tomboy should be the least of his problems, but when she was around, she was the most. And now, instead of heading for the pasture, instead of riding out with the men on horseback, feeling the wind in his face, the sun on his back, he turned and went into the house to check on his "guest," the woman he'd thought would be gone by now, out of his den, out of his life. He sighed loudly. When would life be back to normal?

In the kitchen he made a peanut butter and jelly sandwich on white bread and poured a glass of milk, then walked down the hall. He opened the door with one hand, balancing the tray in the other. She was staring out the window, her back to him, watching the old dog, the one who was too lame to herd anymore, chase a butterfly.

She turned slowly and gazed at him with those wide gray eyes and he wondered, as he did every time he walked into the room, if she'd remembered anything about her past. The strain that etched lines around her mouth told him she hadn't. "Lunchtime," he announced, trying to sound more cheerful than he felt.

"I'm really not..."

"Hungry, I know, but the doctor said..."

"I know what he said, 'eat, drink and relax and your memory will come back to you.'" The corner of her mouth turned down at the sight of the sandwich on the tray.

He set it on her lap anyway. "You don't want me to tell him you're not following orders, do you?" he asked, leaning against the brown-and-yellow plaid wallpaper that covered the den.

"Did you ask him if I could leave?" she asked.

"*You* asked him if you could leave, remember?" He watched her carefully, noticed the way she ran her slender fingers through her dry hair. Wondering if she'd lost her short-term memory, too, wondering if she'd ever recover. More curious about her past than he cared to admit.

"Yes," she said at last. "And he said I could go when my heartbeat is back to normal and my blood pressure comes up. And you said, 'Good God, when will that be?'"

Despite the bitterness that tinged her words, he felt a smile tug at the corners of his mouth. She did a fair imitation of his voice. Actually got the intonation right.

"I guess it's a toss-up as to who wants me out of here more, you or me," she speculated.

"Eat your sandwich."

"I don't want it."

"I'm sorry it's not something more exciting."

"So am I." She glanced up at him. "Sorry," she sighed.

"Forget it."

"If I knew who I was..."

"At least you know your name. If that's your necklace I found next to the remains of your tent."

She picked up the diamond-encrusted gold pendant from the bedside table and turned it over to read the inscription once again. *To Christine from MTT.* "Do I look like the diamond type to you?" she asked.

He hesitated for a moment, trying to picture her in something besides the extra-large men's flannel pajamas she was still wearing. A dress maybe, with the pendant hanging on her pale skin, nestled between her breasts. He took a deep breath. "Sure, why not?"

She shook her head. "You're a terrible liar, you know."

"A terrible cook and a terrible liar," he said, relieved to have the conversation shift back to himself. "Anything else?"

Christine gave him a long steady look. Just when he thought she wasn't going to speak again, she said, "Did you give me a bath the night I came here?"

His spine stiffened against the wall. "I might have," he said carefully. He'd thought—he'd *hoped* her amnesia would have extended that far. As for him, no such luck. He remembered the touch of her skin, the long bare legs, the contours of her breasts, and he was afraid he might never forget.

"Well if you didn't, who did?" she asked.

He shrugged as if it didn't matter, but it did. After years of ignoring women, of telling himself he didn't need one, didn't want one, the image of her in the bath had haunted him every day since. And every night.

A slight flush tinted her pale cheeks. She knew he'd done it. He knew how vulnerable she'd been, lost and alone and almost unconscious. He wanted to reassure her, tell her he hadn't looked, tell her it didn't mean any more to him than lathering a pedigree sheep before taking it to the Grand National. But he couldn't say that. Because it wasn't exactly true.

She turned away from him and studied the stitches on the quilt that covered the guest bed. "I'm hoping one of these days I'll wake up and remember everything. And I'll be my old self again. Instead of cranky and ungrateful, I'll be charming and gracious—or maybe that's asking too much."

Christine waited for his comment, but Parker didn't say anything. Maybe he thought there was no chance of her being anything but what she was. An invalid with no past and no future and hair that resembled deep-fried cotton candy. From time to time she'd catch him looking at her with curiosity and something else she couldn't name. She couldn't help looking back. What woman wouldn't look at a man with his rugged good looks? He had it all, the suntanned skin, the high cheekbones and the deep-set eyes. Maybe all sheep ranchers looked like that. Maybe they all looked like they could lift a two-hundred-pound sheep with one hand and feed an orphaned lamb with the other. Maybe they all had eyes the color of the winter sky and a jaw chiseled out of granite.

"I called the Department of Missing Persons in Denver," she said with a sideways glance at him. "Your father brought me the portable phone and a phone book."

"And?" He crossed his arms over his chest.

"I'm not missing after all. At least, no one's looking for me." She shrugged as if it didn't matter. As if she didn't care that no one even knew she was gone. But the hollow feeling in the pit of her stomach told her she did care.

"So now what?" he asked

"They said I should come in in person. Then they could register me and run me through their computer." She managed a crooked smile. "As if I hadn't been run through enough already. But I have to go. I know that. Someday soon."

"For all you know someone could still be looking for you, your husband, your children," he suggested.

She shook her head. She drew a quick short breath and a piercing sadness caught her by surprise. "I don't have children. I'd know if I did. And if I did I'd never leave them. I couldn't." No children, of that she was sure, but a husband? Who was MTT? She had no idea. She changed the subject. "Did you see the books Doc brought me on amnesia and on lightning?" she asked. "I've been reading up and I want you to know I *am* going to recover and I *am* going to get out of your life." She tried to smile, but something went wrong and a tear trickled down her cheek. Damn, she was sick of being sick. Of being waited on, of being pathetic. Of being undressed and bathed by handsome strangers with warm, calloused hands.

Parker drew his eyebrows together and frowned at her. "There's no hurry," he said.

"Oh, right. I've been here—what, almost a week?— being waited on by you and your father, taking up your den and your time, lying here like a lump, a lump with no past and no future. Just a present."

"Maybe you're trying too hard to remember," he said. "Just relax. It'll come to you."

"What if I don't want it to come to me? Sometimes I'm afraid to remember. Afraid to find out who I was." *Afraid to leave here.* "Oh, well..." She managed a small smile. "It's not your problem."

He nodded. "My problem is finding a new cook. The old one just left."

"Hence the peanut butter sandwich," she said, looking at it balefully.

"I don't think I've ever heard anyone say 'hence' before."

"I don't think I've ever said it before, either. Maybe I was an English teacher."

"Too bad you weren't a cook."

"You mean you'd hire me?"

"I don't hire women."

"Why not?"

"I've got enough trouble without a woman around the place."

"Then why did you say that?"

He crossed his arms over his chest. "Because getting a cook is on my mind. Is that so surprising?"

She shook her head. Not surprising. But tempting. She was getting well, she needed someplace to go, something to do. But she didn't know where to go or what to do. For some reason she didn't want to go to Denver and present herself at the Department of Missing Persons. The idea of finding out who she was scared her. If she could just buy a little time until she was ready to face the past, whatever it was... "What about just temporarily?" she asked.

"No," he said firmly, and glanced at the door.

"I don't blame you. You don't know what I'd do in the kitchen, forget to turn off the oven, forget to put the bay leaf in the osso buco or the grapes in the chicken Veronique, or..."

"Eat your sandwich," he said abruptly.

Dutifully she picked it up and took a bite. He stalked out of the room without another word.

The day dragged by. She picked up a book on lightning the doctor had brought and learned it could have been worse. Much worse. Her brain could have been fried instead of merely scrambled. She learned that the dizziness, the numbness and the headaches were perfectly normal. She read about people who became shamans and healers after they recovered, and she wondered what she'd become and what she'd been, if anything. She felt restless, and useless.

When the doctor came that afternoon, Parker's father brought him to her room and stood in the hall while Doc Haller told her her blood pressure was almost normal and her heart rate steady.

When he left, Parker's father knocked on her door. She looked up as the old man shuffled into the room and stood at the window looking out at the sheep in the shade of the ponderosa pines.

"The doctor says I'm well . . . well enough to leave," she said.

"What ya gonna do?" he asked, turning his head in her direction.

"I'm . . . not sure. Go to Denver, I guess, and check in with the Department of Missing Persons. See if they can find out who I am."

"Maybe your folks will be looking for you."

"Maybe," she acknowledged, though in her heart she knew no one was looking for her. It made her sad to know that, but it gave her a feeling of freedom, freedom to be whoever and whatever she wanted to be. A freedom so immense it scared the living daylights out of her.

"You have a job?"

"I don't know. I suppose I must have...unless..."

Unless somebody else supported her. Somebody... like a husband.

"You *want* a job?" he asked abruptly.

"Yes, but who would hire me? I've got no references, no background, nobody to vouch for me." She gulped. "I don't even have any clothes."

"Suppose we get you some. Suppose you work here."

She smiled a real smile for the first time since she could remember. Her face felt like it might crack under the strain. "As a cook?" she asked hopefully.

He nodded.

Her heart fell. "I can't."

"Why not?"

"Parker doesn't want me here. We already talked about it. I don't blame him. He says women don't belong here."

"He's had some bad experiences," the old man said, slowly lowering himself into the chair by the window. "One very bad experience," he added under his breath.

Christine sat up straight. "I see," she said, hoping he'd elaborate. Maybe it wasn't entirely her fault he was stubborn and hardheaded about her working there. Maybe it wasn't only her he disliked, maybe it was all women because of one certain woman...or something. If only he'd give her a chance. "I'd like to stay awhile," she said to Parker's father. What was his name? Emilio, that was it. "I might not be a good cook, Emilio, but I could give it a try, just until Parker finds a replacement," she said, trying to hide her eagerness, her desperation. "I actually think I might do a good job."

He nodded. "So do I." He rose from the chair by bracing his hands on the armrests. "I'll speak to him."

Christine wondered if anyone could speak to him. Or if he'd listen when they did. When Parker's father left the room she swung her legs over the side of the bed and waited a long moment with her head between her knees until the dizziness stopped. Then she staggered down the hall to the bathroom and ran a bath for herself. She had to show him, to convince him she was no threat. If he was afraid she'd make trouble being the only woman on the place, he only had to look closely, as she was staring into the bathroom mirror, to see that no man would look twice at the battle-scarred creature that looked back at her with wide eyes under singed eyebrows, cracked lips and hair... The less said about her hair, the better. But it was time to wash it and cut the ends off. In the cabinet she found a pair of nail scissors, shampoo and something called Lanolux the Pomade for Purebreds, guaranteed to put a shine in their fleece. She opened the jar and inhaled a clean, lemon waxy scent. She hoped no one would mind if she helped herself. Because if ever she needed a shine in her fleece it was now.

Out behind the house Parker was mixing the ration for the lambs. When his father came around the side of the house, he tilted his hat back on his head and rested his pitchfork on the ground.

"You know if you raised merinos, you wouldn't have to bother with this." His father waved his arm at the bins of grain.

"I wouldn't have to bother selling my lambs for meat, either, would I? I'd be in the wool business. Which I'm not."

"Well, it's yours now," his father said. "Yours to do whatever you want, raise Shropshires, Hampshires or Corriedales, if you want. But if I were you..."

"You'd go back to wool. Pop, eighty percent of sheep money comes from selling lambs. When the pasture was sparse and dry, you had to grow wool. But we've built it up with grass and alfalfa and clover. In a good year we make more money than we can spend. Doesn't it feel good to know you've passed on to me one of the best sheep ranches in the valley?"

His father nodded, then frowned. "Who're *you* going to pass it on to, Sarah?"

"Sarah? Sarah's a girl. Girls—women don't belong on a ranch. You know my feelings on that. Sarah can be a doctor or a lawyer or president of the United States, if she wants. Anything but a rancher. That's one reason I've got her in school in Denver. It's one of the best prep schools in the west. It will open doors for her."

"Seems like the only doors she wants to open are the barn doors."

Parker stiffened. "I know that."

There was a long silence while Parker thought about the whirlwind bundle of energy, the stubborn, determined little girl he'd been struggling to raise since her mother had walked out on them only six months after she was born.

"It's not too late for you to bear a son," his father suggested.

Parker didn't answer. They'd had this conversation before and it went nowhere. Parker had no intention of getting married again or bearing another child. His father knew that, and yet he never gave up.

"Find a cook yet?" his father asked, apparently willing to drop the subject of sons and heirs.

He scowled. "I forgot about it."

"More concerned about feeding your lambs than your hands."

"Maybe."

"I had an idea," Emilo said.

"Don't say you want to hire that woman in there," he said, fixing his father with a disapproving look.

"How d'ya know?"

"I'm psychic. And she already asked me. I said no."

"How come?"

"I don't want any—"

"Women on the ranch, I know, but dinnertime's comin' on and you got nothin' to feed ten or eleven hungry men tonight."

"What about leftovers?"

"They ate 'em for lunch."

"We got a freezer full of meat," Parker suggested.

"You gonna cook it?"

He threw up his hands in disgust. "Okay. One dinner. But I doubt she can remember how to boil an egg."

"Not gonna have eggs."

"No, we're probably going to have osso buco or chicken Veronique," he said dryly.

His father scratched his head. "What's that?"

"Damned if I know."

"You gonna tell her?" Emilio asked his son.

Parker sighed loudly and wiped his hands on his jeans. "Guess I'd better. You'd probably give her a long-term contract and promise her a retirement package in the bargain."

His father smiled faintly. "I'd at least give her a chance."

"I am. I'm giving her a chance."

"She might be a fine-looking woman, underneath it all."

"That's what I'm afraid of," Parker said grimly, and went inside the house.

The kitchen door banged behind him and when his eyes adjusted from the bright sunlight outside, he saw Christine, wearing a pair of large jeans cinched at the waist standing at the stove stirring something that smelled like wine and mushrooms. His mouth fell open and he stood stock-still staring at her.

Startled, she turned to look at him, her gray eyes wide and surprised. But no one was more surprised than he was. First, that she was standing. Second, that she was standing at the stove, and third, her hair. Her once-dry, scorched hair was a lustrous mass of short brown curls framing her face. The sight of her and the smell of whatever she was cooking affected him in the most basic and sensual way. He wanted to break eye contact with her, but he could only stand and stare and imagine what her hair would feel like between his fingers. How she'd react if he suddenly kissed her.

She licked her lips, lips that were once dry and parched and were now moist, full, desirable. Then she spoke. "I, uh, I don't know if he told you, but your father thought I might fill in for you, just temporarily of course." She twisted her fingers together. She was nervous. She ought to be nervous.

"He did? Did he tell you it was just for one night?"

"No, but that's probably all I can do. I mean, the doctor was here this afternoon. I'm fine now. And raring to go." She tried to smile but it came out more like a grimace. "So I will. Go, I mean."

"Where?"

She shrugged. "I'm not sure really."

"How?"

"How? I'll figure it out." She picked up a spoon and turned back to the stove. "If you'll excuse me, I've got to get this sauce right. For the lamb chops.... Is lamb all right? You seem to have an ample supply." She glanced at the door of the walk-in freezer.

"Fine," he said through stiff lips, and walked through the living room and out the front door, knowing without a shadow of a doubt that this was the worst mistake he'd made since his first marriage. He could have said no. He could have said she couldn't cook, not even once, not even one dinner, but what excuse could he give? "You've overstayed your welcome already... I don't want any women on my ranch, especially those who arouse my sympathy and admiration at the same time... And I *really* don't want any women who arouse my lust, who remind me of what's missing in my life." No, those were things he couldn't say, but he couldn't keep from thinking them.

Dinner in the bunkhouse, that two-story structure only yards from the sprawling ranch house, was an unexpectedly jolly event, at least for the ranch hands. All ten of them had gotten the news of the new cook and had shown up at least a half hour ahead of time, hair slicked down and clean shirts despite a hard day rounding up stray lambs and pregnant ewes. Once seated around the table Christine served a green salad dressed with olive oil and lemon, then immediately retreated to the kitchen. Parker barely glanced up at her, hoping the men would follow his example, but that wasn't likely. Their heads swiveled, their mouths fell open, they stared, first at Christine, then when she left, at the pile of green leaves in front of them.

"What's this?"

"Rabbit food."

"Shut up and eat."

"Hey, she the one got hit by lightning?"

"Can't remember what hit her."

"Good lookin' lady anyway."

She came back to collect the salad bowls, every one licked clean, then brought a mound of seasoned rice and lamb chops swimming in the elegant sauce Parker had seen her making, and a platter of green beans garnished with chopped nuts. Where she'd found the ingredients for this dinner Parker had no idea. Of course he hadn't looked into the freezer for some time, either. Again the men were stunned into momentary silence. But only momentary.

"Hey, boss, what's it take to make this lady stay?"

Parker looked up. "I thought you liked *plain* food."

"Thought I did, too, but damned if I'm not changing my mind," Russ said, mopping up the sauce with a crust of French bread.

"So, tell her we want her. Tell her we gotta have her," Jake implored.

"She might not have a memory, but she's got what it takes otherwise," Randy observed with a low chuckle.

Parker frowned. Was the man talking about her cooking, or... Oh, Lord, why had he ever let her cook this dinner? Now he was caught. He glanced at his father who was watching him with a half smile on his face and reaching for another helping of rice at the same time. His father gave him a conspiratorial wink and Parker's heart fell to the soles of his boots. He knew what his father was thinking. See, see how good she is? See how she fits in? Let's keep her. Make her an offer she can't refuse.

Parker also knew it wasn't going to happen. Not if he had anything to say about it. Because a woman like that on a ranch would bring more trouble than they could imagine. He knew. He'd been through it all before.

Chapter Three

After dinner the men eagerly carried their plates to the kitchen while Parker stayed at the table, his elbows propped in front of him, staring off into space. His father, too, stayed where he was absently feeding scraps of bread to the old retired sheepdog who sat at his feet.

"Not too bad, was it, for a first time?" his father asked finally.

"Not bad at all," he admitted. "If she was just a little older, a little..."

"Uglier?"

"That would help."

"Help her get the job?"

"You know where the men are now, don't you?" Parker asked his father. "They're hanging out in the kitchen."

"Givin' her hand with the dishes. What's wrong with that?"

"Nothing. If it stops there, but you know it won't. Next thing you know they're following her down the hall to her room, taking her into town on Saturday nights, getting into fights over who dances with her, hanging around the kitchen instead of working... Yes, I can see it now."

His father looked up. "She don't look like the type who'd encourage the men."

Parker shook his head. Had his father forgotten already?

"I know what you're thinkin'. Neither did Cheryl. But this is not your wife, this is a cook."

Parker stood. "That's *not* what I was thinking. I haven't thought about Cheryl for years. I'm thinking of what's best for the ranch. For the men. For my sanity."

"Food's important," his father noted.

"Of course it's important. I'm not going to let the men starve. The agency promised me someone tomorrow. I'm going in to interview him, whoever it is, and if he's halfway decent, I'll bring him back with me."

"What about her?"

Parker exhaled loudly. "What about her? She's not my responsibility anymore. I've done all I can for her. Found her, fed her and got her well. Now it's time for her to move on. To go home. She has a home you know."

"You saved her life," his father noted. "You know what that means when you save someone's life. They belong to you."

"Pop, what's gotten into you? She doesn't belong to me, she belongs to somebody else, somewhere else. For all we know they're out of their minds with worry over what's happened to her."

"You would be, wouldn't you?" his father asked.

"How do I know? She *doesn't* belong to me. And she doesn't belong here. I saved her life, she cooked us dinner. Now we're even."

"One fine dinner," his father added. "You have to admit that."

Parker exhaled loudly and rocked back on his heels. "You want her to stay, don't you? You want me to call the agency and tell them we've got a cook. But I'm not going to do that. I've got to do what's best for the ranch. And having an attractive woman around is definitely not it." He met his father's gaze head-on. It was not the first time they'd disagreed and it wouldn't be the last. He recognized the stubborn set of his father's chin, the determined look in his eyes. "I'm not always right, Pop, I know that. But you've got to trust me on this one. Women make trouble. They may not want to, it may not be their fault at all, but sooner or later it happens."

His father sighed heavily and got to his feet. "Your mother never made any trouble," he said, "but it's your ranch now. Not mine. You make the decisions. I was only trying to help."

"You do help," Parker insisted. "I value your advice, your experience. But..."

"Never mind," the old man said with a wave of his hand. "Do what you think is best."

Parker nodded and left the dining room. He headed off in the opposite direction from the house toward the barn where he went through the motions of checking pregnant ewes for irregular fetal positions, spreading fresh straw in the pens, but his mind was back at the house, thinking of Christine, going over his conversation with her. She knew she was leaving tomorrow. She said one night was all she could do, she said she was "raring to go." She didn't *want* to stay any longer. That's what his father didn't understand. And neither did the boys. After he killed some more time adding protein supplement to the animals' feed, he ambled back toward the house.

The kitchen was dark, the house was quiet. He breathed a sigh of relief. Why should he care if the boys wanted to hang around the kitchen after dinner one night? It's not like it was going to be a problem. She'd leave tomorrow and he'd get a new cook, a man. No women on the place, no problems. Of course, his mother hadn't made any trouble. It was just the two of them in those days, the two of them working together and a small herd of sheep. Then he was born and his mother died. He never knew her, maybe that's why he had such a hard time with women. He'd grown up with men, his father and the ranch hands. The only exception in all these years was Sarah's nanny, a fifty-something, good-hearted woman named Mrs. Dodge, who was five feet two inches tall and weighed about one hundred seventy-five pounds. When Mrs. Dodge finally left to care for her ailing mother, Sarah went off to boarding school. And things had been fine ever since. Until now.

He found himself walking down the hall toward the den. He rapped lightly on the door and when she didn't answer, he pushed the door open. The room was empty. He stood staring into the darkness, at the empty bed, his heart beating just a little bit faster.

He turned and walked briskly back down the hall, through the living room and out into the cool night air onto the wide, old-fashioned front porch. She was there. He hadn't realized he was holding his breath until he heard the creak of the old wooden swing as it swayed back and forth. She didn't turn, but she dug the toe of her shoe into the floorboard and the swing came to a stop.

Casually, so she wouldn't think he'd been looking for her, he sauntered across the porch and leaned against the post that supported the overhang. "You don't need me to tell you," he said with a glance in her direction, "that the dinner was good, very good."

"It's always nice to hear a compliment," she said.

"You must have heard many," he said with a glance at the oversize white shirt she wore and the faint outline of her features he made out as his eyes grew accustomed to the darkness.

"Not really," she said with a rueful look at the jeans held together by a belt tied at the waist. "Oh, you mean in my other life. I don't know about that."

"Nothing yet? No clue as to what you were? If tonight is any indication, you've had some experience cooking."

"I suppose so. It came to me as I was doing it—what to put in the sauce, how long to cook the meat, but I don't know how I knew." She frowned.

"I was thinking," he said after a brief pause. Might as well get it settled tonight. "I could give you a ride into town tomorrow. There's an afternoon bus to Denver. I'll get you a ticket, of course."

"I can't..."

"You can pay me back," he continued. "You'll need something to wear, too. There's a dry goods store in town, nothing fancy, but it'll be better than nothing."

"I guess so, but isn't there another way to town?" she asked. "I hate to take you away from your work."

"I have to go in anyway, pick up the new cook."

"Oh...yes, I see. Well in that case..."

"If you're well enough to go," he said, feeling a sharp prick of conscience. What if she fainted on the bus? What if she forgot to get off at the right stop?

"Of course I'm well enough," she said brightly. "I'm as good as new. In fact, it's like being new, having no memory. Everything I do, it's as if I'm doing it for the first time, and yet..." There was a long silence while he waited for her to continue her thought, but she didn't. "It was fun cooking. I felt useful for the first time since...you know... It got my mind off myself... what mind is left that is," she added with a half smile. Then she stood. "Good night," she said abruptly, and she went into the house.

He stood staring at the front door. Surprised at how easy it had been. He didn't know what he'd expected. She might have protested, said she wasn't well enough to travel. She could have asked for a chance to stay on permanently. Maybe she really was ready to go. Maybe she wanted to leave as much as he wanted her to. That must be it. Yes, tomorrow everything would be back to normal. He was looking forward to that. He really was.

In the night the smell of flowers came and choked off the air around her. The bouquet of white roses, the centerpieces of pale yellow freesias that matched the dresses came to surround her, press in on her. Once so sweet, now cloying, suffocating. Christine sat up in bed and gasped for air, throwing the blanket off the daybed with shaking fingers. The white satin dress encrusted with pearls fit like a glove, a glove too tight, too small, too confining. She had to take it off, but she couldn't reach the tiny buttons that marched down the back. Panicky, she yanked at the flannel pajamas that hung on her slender frame. She looked down and forced herself to breathe deeply. There was no dress. There were no flowers. She was in the guest room at the Robinson Ranch. She was safe, for now. But tomorrow she would have to face the past, a past so sad she could only remember it in nightmares.

She buried her face in her hands and sobbed. What was wrong with her that the smell of flowers should remind her of something so sad she couldn't stop crying? Why should a beautiful wedding dress be the cause of a nightmare? Weddings were happy affairs, filled with love and laughter. Not this one. Not this time.

Gradually the tears dried on her cheeks, but underneath, a sadness too deep for tears wouldn't go away. She covered herself with the blanket and lay down again, but sleep refused to come back. The thought of leaving the ranch to go back to her old life terrified her. She didn't know why, she just knew she was better off where she was. But better or not, she was leaving tomorrow. Or rather today, she thought with a rueful glance at the clock.

In the middle of the morning Parker brought his truck around to the front of the house, told his father he was going, knocked on the door of the den, heard her answer, then went out to the truck to wait impatiently. The sooner they got this over with, the better.

When Christine finally came out, she was wearing the same extra-large jeans, a man's shirt and pair of unisex athletic shoes. He didn't ask where any of it had come from. He didn't want to know.

"Sorry I'm late," she said, reaching for the passenger door. "I wanted to say goodbye to your father."

"No hurry," he said, turning the key in the ignition. Just take your time. Say goodbye to my father, why not to the rest of the boys, too? Plenty of time.

"He's such a nice man."

He knew what she meant. *He's* such a nice man. What happened to you? "He's been at it a long time," he explained, grateful to have a subject for conversation. "Came out here and homesteaded with my mother. Maybe he told you."

"He's had quite a life, full of ups and downs."

Parker knew what one of the major downs was. "I'm somewhat of a disappointment to him," he said.

She turned to look at him. "That's not what he said."

"What did he say?" Parker asked, genuinely curious.

"He's worried about you. He thinks you ought to get married."

"Did he tell you I've been married?"

Her eyes widened. "No."

"That I have a twelve-year-old daughter?"

"You do? Where is she? Why didn't I see her?"

"She goes to school in Denver. Local schools are no good. I know, I went to them."

"I see," she said thoughtfully. "I wish...I could have met her."

"You like kids?"

"Yes."

"Then why..."

"Why don't I have any? I don't know." She stared out the window. "Maybe I'm not married." She held up her hand. "No ring."

She didn't have to tell him. He'd noticed. "Maybe you left it behind. All I know is, anybody who looks like *you* and *cooks* like you is probably married."

She smiled faintly. "I guess that's a compliment."

He shook his head. "Just an observation."

She shot a swift glance in his direction. "I could say the same about you. Anybody who looks like *you* is probably married. But you're not. That's not a compliment, by the way. Just an observation."

He bit back a grin, fought off the urge to say "touché," then focused on the long ribbon of road ahead. It was better to count telephone poles than to have a personal discussion.

Christine wished she hadn't said that. Yes, he was good-looking. Today with a fresh shirt that matched the blue of his eyes and clean, well-worn jeans that hugged his narrow hips, she could hardly tear her eyes away from him. But what was the point of letting him know she noticed? In a few hours she'd never see him again. He'd be on his way back to the ranch with a new cook. She'd be on a bus for Denver, back to her old life. Her real life. The thought terrified her. She would rather jump off a speeding train or go back into a coma. But why? What was it back there that was so bad? Maybe it was time to find out. On the other hand, maybe it wasn't.

It was strange how much at home she felt on the ranch. How comfortable. Despite Parker who made her feel something, but not comfortable. He puzzled her, intrigued her, and yes, attracted her. There were moments when she thought it might be mutual. But maybe not. He didn't want her around anymore. But the kind old man did. He thought she ought to stay on and cook. If it weren't for Parker she could have. But if it weren't for Parker, she'd be lying in the middle of that pasture with the vultures nibbling on her bones. She sighed.

He looked at her. "Tired?"

"Just a little nervous. How would you feel if you were about to uncover your past?"

"Terrible."

"Was it so bad?"

"Well . . ." he said, deliberately avoiding her question as he slowed his truck and rolled down his window. "Here we are. Welcome to Clear Creek. Once a thriving mining town, now mostly ranchers."

Christine looked out the side window at narrow streets, plank sidewalks and some carefully restored buildings. She should have known better than to ask a question about his past. He wasn't going to tell her anything.

"And there's the general store I was telling you about." He gave her a sidelong glance. "They ought to have something to fit you. Just tell them to put it on my charge."

"I don't like to do that."

"You can't wear those clothes in Denver."

She looked down at the rolled-up cuffs of her pants. "Pretty ridiculous, huh? I'll pay you back," she assured him.

He parked in front of the store, reached across her and opened her door for her. His arm brushed her breasts. Accidentally. For some reason she suddenly remembered the night he'd undressed her. She sucked in a quick breath.

He cleared his throat. "I'll meet you back here in an hour."

She nodded and slowly got out of the truck. She knew he was going to the agency to interview the new cook. Why it hurt so much to be replaced by an anonymous man, she didn't know. It wasn't as if she wanted the job. It wasn't as if she could stay on at the ranch and just ignore the fact that she had no memory. She had to face her past sooner or later. It was just that she'd rather it was later.

As she walked across the planked pavement a ripple of awareness ran up her spine. Without turning she knew he was watching her. Instead of hurrying to the agency he was sitting in his truck with his eyes on her. She opened the door to the dry goods store and reminded herself that he *wanted* her to go. She told herself there was no way she could stay. Not unless... She forced herself to stop dreaming and face reality. The smell of denim and leather filled the air. Stacks of blue jeans lined the walls in every style and every size. Felt hats hung from racks and in the back of the store was the shoe and boot department.

A middle-aged saleswoman who wore relaxed-fit jeans, a red-and-white checkered shirt and leather boots took one look at Christine and smiled knowingly. "The works, right?" she asked.

"Something I can wear in the city as well as..." As well as what? She was going to the city, period. She was never coming back there. She didn't finish her sentence. She didn't have to. The woman seemed to know exactly what she wanted.

It wasn't long before Christine was outfitted in smooth, soft, prewashed denims that hugged her hips, an off-white, all-cotton shirt and a pair of suede boots. To ward off the chill spring breeze, she bought a lightweight fitted jacket. And just in case it took a while to find out who she was in Denver, she bought some extra cotton underwear, jeans and shirts. As the woman totaled the bill she wondered how and when she'd pay Parker back.

The saleswoman looked up in surprise when Christine told her to put it on his bill.

"He does have a charge account here, doesn't he?" Christine asked anxiously.

"Oh, yes, of course. I was just wondering... You're the lady who's been staying out at the ranch, the one who was struck by lightning?"

She should have known. It was a small town. "Yes, that's me. But I'm fine now. On my way home, in fact."

"I heard you...you lost your memory, is that right?" The woman stood on the other side of the counter with her pencil poised, the amount of the bill still untotaled.

Christine nodded. What could she say?

"My cousin Luke shears for them. He went out just before lambing. Says Parker's a good man to work for. Fair and honest. Always pays right on time."

Christine nodded and looked at the unfinished bill on the counter. "I'll bet he does."

"'Course, the women in town are more interested in his looks and his money. Not a one of them who wouldn't like to cheer him up, make him forget about Cheryl. Be a mother to poor little Sarah. But no such luck." She paused. "I guess it's the kind of thing you never forget. From the day his wife left the only woman ever to work there was dear old Mrs. Dodge, Sarah's nanny. Don't think they didn't try though. Practically lined up on the front porch wanting to cook for him, clean for him, teach his daughter to play the piano or speak French. Maybe that's one reason he sent her away to school. Well, anyway..." she said, finally ringing up the sale on her cash register. "You get the picture."

Christine got the picture. The picture of herself at the end of a long line of applicants, of women trying to get their foot in the door to make a play for the town's most eligible bachelor. She put her packages under her arm, said goodbye and walked out the door. There on the sidewalk, leaning against a hitching post, was Parker, his hat shading his face from the sun shining from a cloudless sky.

When he saw her he did a double take. "Well," he said with a long look that started at the top of her head and ended with her new boots. "You did all right."

"I'm afraid I spent a lot of your money, but I'll..."

"Pay me back, I know," he said brusquely, tearing his eyes away from her to glance across the street at a café advertising home-cooked food. "I picked up your bus ticket. It doesn't leave until two. I don't know about you, but I didn't have breakfast this morning. I'm ready for lunch."

She shifted the packages from one arm to the other. This was going too far. First the ride to town, then the clothes and now lunch. It was time to break it off. Now. "I don't think so."

He jerked his head back to look at her. "What do you mean?" He took a step forward until his face was inches from hers, until she could see into the depths of his blue eyes. "Aren't you hungry? Are you sick?"

She licked her lips, hoping she'd be able to speak, to come up with an excuse, but all she could do was shake her head. He took the packages from under her arm, then grasped her elbow firmly and led her across the street. "Then you'll eat. *We'll* eat."

The place was packed. As they passed crowded booths on their way to the back of the restaurant, people called out.

"Hey, Parker."

"What's doin'?"

"How's things?"

She was only too aware of their curious glances in her direction, but he kept moving, his hand exerting a firm pressure on the small of her back, until they were settled in the last booth in the corner.

She rested her elbows on the table and looked at him. Seeing him through the eyes of the townspeople, the women who wanted him, the men who liked him. No wonder her heart was beating double time. He was an enigma, a challenge, a man with a past, where she had none. A man who hid his feelings, if he had any.

He looked up. "What?" he asked, startled by the awareness in her eyes.

"Nothing." She picked up her menu and hid behind it. "The Western omelet sounds good."

Parker continued to look at her, at what he could see behind that menu, at her shoulders, the sleeves of her new shirt, at her fingers, slender and ringless. He had to grip the edge of the table to keep from taking the menu out of her hands and looking into those wide gray eyes again, just to catch a glimpse of whatever it was he saw. But he wasn't going to do anything rash. Not now. Not ever. And he wasn't going to offer her the job, not if they had to eat peanut butter sandwiches from now to eternity.

As if she'd read his thoughts, she set her menu down and said, "How did it go? The cook," she reminded him. "Was he okay?"

"No," he said shortly. "He wasn't. He'd been fired at the last two places for stealing the silverware."

Her eyes widened. The waitress came. They ordered. He stared off into space over her head. She unfolded her napkin. "That's too bad," she said.

"He was a good cook though. They all vouched for his cooking," he volunteered.

"What are you going to do?" she asked.

"Go back after lunch. Keep at it until they find me someone."

She nodded and the food came; his hot roast beef sandwich and her omelet with toast and hash browns. He watched her down her glass of milk and wondered where she'd be eating dinner tonight. At the head of a long table in some high-ceilinged dining room, with her long-lost family, or in one of those restaurants downtown where they carve the meat at your table? Or would she never get out of the Greyhound bus station, would she wander around lost and confused, unable to find her way to the Department of Missing Persons?

When they finished, he frowned and left money on the table. Then he took her to the bus stop, pressed some money into her hand and gave her her ticket and her package of new clothes. She looked calm and competent. There was nothing to worry about.

"Thanks again," she said with a quick smile. Did her lower lip tremble or was that his imagination?

"You're welcome." He kissed her on the cheek, tipped his hat and turned and walked away. Told himself it wasn't as bad as he'd imagined. She'd be fine. He kicked a stone the size of a small boulder off the road next to his truck and winced as the pain shot through his foot. Yes, she'd be fine. But would he?

Chapter Four

Parker went back to the agency and restlessly thumbed through the files. He tossed the folders back across the desk. "Nothing. There's nobody I could even interview," he explained.

"Sorry about that, Mr. Robinson," the woman said. "A good cook is always in demand, man or woman. But I may have something next week. Why don't you check back with me then?"

"Next week? What am I supposed to do till then?" he grumbled, getting to his feet. "My men have got to eat."

She shrugged as if it wasn't her problem, which it wasn't. Parker walked out of the office. He stood out in front staring at his truck, knowing he couldn't go home and face the men without a cook. He couldn't ask them to work as hard as they did without a hearty breakfast or a good meal to look forward to at the end of the day. Without knowing where he was going he started walking, past the feed and fuel store, past the grange, the university extension agriculture office, and around the block.

He looked at his watch. A few minutes past two o'clock. His mind was spinning, picturing her face in the bus window, the lost look in her eyes, her lower lip trembling. Impulsively, he turned and ran toward the bus station. The bus for Denver was just pulling away. He sprinted after it, not knowing what he'd do if he caught it. It stopped to let a car pass and he peered in the windows one by one. She wasn't there. He ran behind the bus and canvassed the passengers on the other side. There was nobody with short brown curly hair and gray eyes and wearing new clothes. Where was she?

He should never have let her go by herself. No matter what she said, he realized she still needed help. He should have taken her to the bus and made sure she got on it. Was she lost and wandering around somewhere? Damn it, where was she? How far could she have gotten? He got in his truck and cruised the narrow streets of Clear Creek, originally built for horse-drawn traffic, his fingers gripping the steering wheel, his gaze sweeping the quiet neighborhoods. In front of the grade school a bell rang. The crossing guard signaled him to stop. Children crossed the street in front of him. He rolled his window down.

Impatiently he ran his hand through his hair. Then he saw her, standing at the fence, her gaze fixed on the children as they poured out the front door.

Keeping one eye on Christine, he parked the truck across from the school and crossed the street. As he approached he realized her gaze was so intent on the children she was unaware of anything else, especially him. He stood a few feet away, watching her watch the kids with an unmistakable look of longing in her eyes.

"Christine?"

She turned toward him and he was stunned by the look of sadness mingled with the longing. "What's wrong?" he demanded.

With obvious effort, she drew a long, shaky breath and wiped at the tears that threatened to spill out of her eyes. "Hello, Parker," she said, giving him a tremulous smile.

"Why weren't you on the bus? Why aren't you on your way to Denver?"

"I am, I am..." she said. Then she frowned. "Why aren't you on your way home?"

"Because..." He grabbed her by the shoulders. "I was worried about you. You weren't on the bus. Damn it, Christine..." He wanted to shake her, to tell her he couldn't leave not knowing where she was, but instead he bent his head and kissed her. If she was surprised, he was even more surprised. He had no intention of kissing her in front of the Clear Creek elementary school or anywhere for that matter.

But once his lips met hers he forgot where he was. Forgot everything but how her lips tasted and how fragile she felt in his arms. Her arms tightened around him as if he was her anchor. He wasn't. He wasn't her anything. And yet for one crazy moment he wanted to be. Wanted her to lean on him, to depend on him. To throw her arms around him and kiss him as if she wanted him as much as he wanted her.

But instead she pulled back and gave him a questioning look under her long lashes. There was a long silence where neither knew what to say. Then she took a deep breath. "There was no need to worry. I decided to take the later bus. So you can go on home."

"I can't go home without a cook," he said grimly, dropping his arms to his sides.

"Still no cook?"

He shook his head. He let his eyes drift down her prewashed jeans to her new suede boots, and then back up to her windbreaker jacket until he finally met her gaze again. "What time's your bus?" he inquired, stifling the urge to tell her not to leave.

She ran her hand through her hair. "Five, I think, or maybe later."

"Later? Any later and you'll wind up at the bus station after dark." He clenched his hands into fists thinking of her wandering around the city after dark.

"I suppose so," she admitted.

"You can't do that. It's too dangerous. What is wrong with you? Did the lightning knock all the sense out of you?"

She shrugged, unoffended by his harsh words. "If it did, it'll come back along with my memory." She picked up her shopping bag and turned to leave, as if he wasn't even there.

He took her by the arm. Lord, she was maddening. "You think I'm going to let you leave without any sense or any memory?" he demanded. "I don't know what you'd do, where you'd end up."

His strong grip on her arm made her tremble inside. She was still reeling from his kiss. She wanted to throw herself back into his arms and never leave. Then she'd never have to face the past. But she'd never have a future unless she found her past. "I'll let you know," she promised, lifting her chin a notch. "I'll send you a card."

"That's great. What am I supposed to do in the meantime?"

She drew her eyebrows together. Was he worried? About her? Hardly. "Take care of your sheep, I suppose," she suggested lightly.

"I wish I could." He sighed loudly. "Oh, hell," he said. "You might as well come back with me."

She blinked. "Back with you?" she repeated. "You don't want any women around, remember? I'm a woman."

"I know," he said tersely. "But it can't be helped. I need a cook, you need a place to go. Temporarily."

She sighed. She'd almost worked up enough nerve to leave and now he was offering a way to stay. Offering? More like ordering. She stood there, teetering on the fence. Should she go or should she stay?

She took a deep breath. She couldn't resist. "As long nas it's only temporary," she said. "Because sooner or later I've got to go, you know."

"And sooner or later I've got to find a permanent cook, but for now, I really have no choice."

"Thanks," she said dryly, realizing that she wasn't going to get much more than that from him in the way of kind words or persuasion. He knew she didn't have much choice, either.

"Of course I'd pay you the going rate."

She nodded. "Then I can pay you back for the clothes."

It gave him an excuse to look at her clothes again, the ones he'd bought her. She felt the heat of his gaze as his eyes lingered on the open jacket, then on the buttons that marched down the front of her shirt, and her face flushed under his scrutiny. The memory of his undress ing her that first day lingered in her mind, even though she was barely conscious at the time. She had the feeling he'd seen more than just her bruised and battered body. He'd seen into her soul. He'd seen into her heart.

All he really knew about her was what she knew. That she was a woman who needed a place to go. As his gaze lingered she almost felt him undressing her again, but this time lazily, sensuously, as if he had all afternoon. She must be going crazy. She told herself Parker Robinson was not interested in her as a woman, just as a cook, and only out of desperation. She was misconstruing the look he gave her. Reading more into it than was there. But she zipped her jacket up to her chin anyway, intending to move, to cross the street to the truck, but her feet wouldn't budge, her legs wouldn't obey her feeble brain. Was it him or had all men had this effect on her—of turning her insides to mush with a look or a touch? Why couldn't she remember?

Finally he took her firmly by the arm and led her to his truck, as if he was afraid she might change her mind. Or he might change his. They drove in silence for a long while, each wondering if they'd done the right thing, neither wanting to admit it. But when they stopped at a grocery store, they had something to talk about, something concrete to discuss.

"Plain meat and potatoes," he said as he walked behind her past the produce. "Nothing Veronique or buco or anything."

She sighed. "You know you may be underestimating the men. They seem to have the capacity to appreciate something more than meat and potatoes."

Briskly she continued filling her basket with potatoes, carrots and onions, then moved on to staples like flour and sugar and a big bag of rice.

"Mostly women in here," he noted with a frown.

"Does that bother you?" she asked, realizing he was right, and that the women were giving him more than a passing glance. She could understand why. He'd stand out anywhere with his broad shoulders, narrow hips and ruggedly handsome face. And in the middle of a grocery store, he was drawing his share of admiring second looks. She tore her gaze away. She had no wish to be part of his crowd of admirers.

"Let's say I'll be glad to get home," he said.

Home. That word again. Why couldn't she bring forth an image to go with the word? She looked out the side window as they drove down the highway, knowing the answer was not there in the hay and wheat fields. The answer was in Denver. And she was running away from it. "I should have gotten on that bus," she said in a half whisper.

He didn't say anything. He probably wished she had gotten on it. Then she felt his hand on her shoulder, strong, warm, comforting, radiating heat all the way to her heart. "There'll be another one along," he said in his deep voice. "Whenever you're ready."

She nodded, wishing she had the nerve to put her head on his shoulder, to feel his arms around her, and pour out her worst fears. Tell him she was afraid she'd never be ready. But she couldn't do that. He'd been taking care of her for over a week now and all he needed was for her to throw herself in his arms, cry on his shoulder, and he'd turn the truck around and put her on that bus, cook or no cook.

He took his hand away and she bit her lip. The sense of loss hit her like a bale of hay. "You know I don't usually hire women," he said, his voice under strain now.

She turned to look at him. "I know, but..."

"There's a reason for that."

Finally, he was going to tell her. She held her breath.

"They're disruptive."

"In what way?"

"They distract the men from their work."

"I see," she said, but she didn't. Did this have to do with his wife or was it something else entirely? His father's words came back to her. "One very bad experience," he'd said. She knotted her fingers together, waiting for Parker to go on.

"When there's a woman on the place, the men hang around the kitchen. Instead of cooperating, which they have to do on a ranch, they compete with each other. Am I making myself clear?"

"Are you saying this is what happened, or what you're afraid might happen?"

"Both. It *has* happened and it might very well happen again. Unless we take precautions." He slanted a look in her direction. A stern look that made her shiver despite the warmth of her jacket.

When she served the dinner that night Christine was more nervous than the first time. She didn't know why. She knew Parker needed her as much as she needed this job. That's the only reason she was there. She put a large casserole of chicken baked with broccoli in a cheese sauce on a tray, along with hot rolls, and coleslaw. She heard the voices and the raucous laughter as she approached the bunkhouse dining room, but the room fell silent as she entered. Despite her plan to appear as modest as a nineteenth century serving girl with downcast eyes, she looked up, startled.

The men looked anywhere but at her. Her eyes widened in surprise. Parker's father, at the far end of the table, smiled at her. Despite her warning, she smiled back, grateful for the emotional support. Surely Parker could have no objection to that. But she couldn't see his face, his back was to her. She left the dining room as fast as possible and the laughter and conversation resumed as if by magic.

She served coffee and rice pudding to the men, then retreated quickly to the kitchen. With her elbows propped on the kitchen table, her chin in her hands, she waited for them to finish eating so she could clear the table. Her eyelids were heavy, her shoulders slumped. She'd only been to Clear Creek and back, but it had been more than that. It had been a chance to journey to the past—and she'd retreated. Failed. She heard footsteps and then the kitchen door opened.

"What's wrong?" Parker sounded alarmed.

She raised her head and tried to smile reassuringly. "Nothing. Just a little tired."

"You should be. Go to bed. I'll get the boys to clear the table and I'll load the dishwasher."

She braced her hand on the table. "I can do it. I'm the cook. And the dishwasher. That's what you're paying me for."

"I'm getting my money's worth," he said, standing in front of the refrigerator. "That was excellent rice pudding."

"Really?"

"Didn't you have any?"

She shook her head.

He looked around the kitchen at the bowls stacked in the sink, the pots and pans still on the stove. "Did you have *anything?*" he demanded.

"Not really."

"Good God, what's wrong with you anyway? No wonder you look like something the cat dragged in." He reached into the cupboard for a plate, piled chicken and broccoli on it and shoved it into the microwave oven. He didn't speak, he just stood watching it until it was hot, then he set it in front of her and said, "Eat."

She straightened and looked up at him. "Haven't we been through this before?"

"With a peanut butter sandwich," he agreed. "At least your short-term memory is still intact." He gave her a knife and fork, then he sat across the table from her in a straight-backed kitchen chair. "Do you want me to cut your meat for you?"

"I'm not a child," she informed him, picking up her fork in one hand, the knife in the other.

"I'm aware of that," he said stiffly. Too much aware. Aware of her desirable body, her luminous gray eyes, the half smile that curved her sensuous lips. Aware that he was in danger, even now, of breaking every one of the rules he'd laid down to the men. Wondering if that was why he'd laid those rules down. So he could have her for himself.

Maybe his interest in her was nothing more than his feeling sorry for her. That he was worried about her. Maybe as soon as she was well, really well, he could put her out of his mind. Out of his house and then out of his mind. Because while she was there he knew he was going to think about her, think up excuses to see her, talk to her, touch her. Even now as he watched her pretend to eat, he wanted to cup her face between his hands, kiss her to see if she'd respond. See if the occasional gleam in her eye had anything to do with passion.

If it was there, he wanted to be the one to awaken it. He wanted to carry her off to bed, not the narrow daybed in the den, but upstairs to the master bedroom. Peel her clothes off once again, only this time she'd know exactly what he was doing. She might even help. He could feel the heat roll through his body, his desire threatening to betray him.

She finally took a few bites of chicken and then looked up at him. He shoved his chair forward. Just because she'd lost her memory didn't mean she'd lost her sight. In the past he'd been transparent. Wearing his heart on his sleeve. Cheryl had used it against him. Never again would he let himself be vulnerable.

"How'd I do?" she asked.

"Do? Oh, all right. Now, go to bed," he said brusquely.

She nodded and got up from the table but held on to the back of her chair for support. He wanted to take her in his arms. Hold her. Steady her. But he didn't. He stayed where he was, feet planted firmly on the tiled floor. He couldn't take advantage of her, not now when she was alone and tired and vulnerable.

"Parker, I just want to thank you..."

"Don't." He didn't want her gratitude. But that was all he was going to get.

"Where would I be without you?"

He shrugged. "Back where you belong, maybe. I don't know." But all he could think was that she belonged right here, in his kitchen. The way she looked around at the open shelves, the oak highboy, made him think she thought so, too. But once her memory came back, she'd be gone, back to where she belonged, to whomever she belonged to. He wasn't kidding. Anybody who looked like her belonged to somebody. "Anyway I'm the one who's thankful."

"For the dinner?"

"Yeah, the dinner. And for saving my life. The boys had mutiny on their minds when I caught up with them. If I hadn't come back with a cook, they would have had my head."

She studied his face for a long moment, her head tilted slightly to one side. "That would have been too bad. It looks good where it is."

It was ridiculous. It wasn't meant as a compliment, but he felt the heat rise up the back of his neck and turn his ears red. "I thought you were going to bed," he said, hoping she wouldn't notice the effect she had on him.

"I can't." She looked around the kitchen at the dirty dishes and took a step in the direction of the large double sink.

He moved to block her. There was no way he was going to let her do those dishes. She ran into him. And before he knew it he had his arms around her, pressing her to him, all the day's tension released in one moment. The one moment he'd been thinking about non-stop since she'd come into his life. He felt her catch her breath, heard her surprised gasp and then felt her body mesh with his. Every soft curve of hers met every hard plane of his and found a home. She looked up and he saw the questions in her eyes. Questions he could only answer with a hard, hungry, soul-searching kiss. Then her lips molded to his, as if they'd done it all before, so familiar and yet so new it made his heart pound.

She put everything into that kiss, as if it was the last. She gave as much as she took from him. Taking and giving. Tasting and savoring. Her generosity touched him. Her sweetness overwhelmed him and made him want more. He forgot everything—where he was and what he promised himself wouldn't happen. Not under his roof. He staggered backward, pulling her with him. Until he backed into the refrigerator. He braced himself against it. His hands cupped the firm contours of her fanny, pulled her against the lean hardness of his body. God, how he wanted her. He'd wanted her since the day he'd found her. Was it possible she wanted him as much? What did it matter? He couldn't have her.

There was a knock on the back door. She jerked out of his arms. He was breathing hard, like a long-distance runner, one who was desperately out of shape. How appropriate. As a lover he was even more out of shape.

"Hope I'm not interrupting anything," Duke, Parker's newest wrangler, said, squinting in the brightly lighted kitchen.

"Of course not," Parker said. "I was just... complimenting the cook."

"No kidding? That's what I wanted to do, if it's okay with you, boss," he said with a shy smile. "Mighty fine meal, ma'am."

"You're welcome... I mean, th-thank you," Christine stammered. "Would you like some more coffee?"

"Coffee's in the bunkhouse," Parker said pointedly.

"Some more pudding?" Christine asked Duke nervously.

What was wrong with her? Parker thought. Couldn't she see how much he wanted to get rid of the guy? How this was the very thing he wanted to avoid? Parker hoped Duke didn't notice how flushed her cheeks were, how red her lips, how her voice shook just slightly. How much had he seen, or merely guessed?

The door opened again and his father walked in. Parker stifled a groan. His eyes met Christine's and he thought he saw a flicker of amusement there. But he wasn't amused. He was annoyed, embarrassed and angry with himself for giving in to lust. That's all it was, unbridled lust looming after all these years of celibacy. Easy to understand, not so easy to control. But he would, by God he'd have to, because on a place like this, everybody knew everything about everybody, and if they didn't, they made it up.

"The kitchen," his father said, looking around at the well-worn surfaces, the old dishes that had served the family for years. "The heart of the place." He smiled. "Just like old times."

Parker didn't know which old times his father was talking about, all he knew was he had to get Christine out of there. Fast. "Good night," he said, giving her a pointed look.

She gave him an inquiring look.

"There are three of us now. We'll have everything cleaned up in minutes. *Good night,*" he repeated.

Without a word she walked out of the room and her footsteps echoed down the hall in the silence that followed. His father looked at him and he looked at Duke, and without any further discussion the two younger men had everything in the dishwasher within minutes. Parker said good-night to his father and walked out the front door to the barn to check on the animals.

But his mind wasn't on the animals. He relived the scene in the kitchen over and over, feeling more like a hypocrite each time he thought about using her to satisfy his lust. That's all it was, he told himself again. And he couldn't sleep until he'd apologized to her. He turned and went back to the house, walking as lightly as he could down the hall to the den. He rapped softly on the door.

"Yes?"

He pushed the door open just slightly. She was in bed, the lamplight shining on her hair, the soft curls that framed her face. She didn't look surprised to see him. But she didn't look exactly happy, either. He stepped inside and carefully closed the door.

"I just wanted to say I'm sorry," he said, leaning against the door. No matter what happened, he was not going any farther into the room. Not even if she was wearing a silk negligee instead of those damned flannel pajamas. Not even if she begged him, pleaded with him.

"For what? Bringing me back here? Telling me I had no sense?"

"No."

She sat there calmly waiting, forcing him to explain when she knew perfectly well what he was talking about. Then for some reason she gave him a break. "You're sorry about what happened in the kitchen, aren't you?"

"Aren't you?" he asked.

"No," she said. "Unless it comes under the category of flirting or encouraging the men, which includes you, I guess."

"No, no, of course not. It was all my fault. You didn't do anything..." Nothing but kiss him like she meant it, look at him with desire in her eyes. "Well, that's all I wanted to say." So it was no big deal for her. He was relieved. Not disappointed. Not at all. "Good night. Again." He said the words but he didn't leave. He just stood there at the door looking at her, aching to cross the room to kiss her again, to see if he could make the magic happen again. To lose himself in her arms. To recover something he'd lost years ago.

She raised her eyebrows inquiringly and he took a deep breath. "I don't want to take advantage of you, of your situation," he said.

She waited, holding perfectly still. The whole house was still, waiting. Waiting for him to spit it out.

He tried again. "I don't want you to think that just because I'm your boss..."

"That I have to exchange sexual favors for your giving me the job."

He stiffened. "That's one way of putting it."

She sat up straight. She *was* wearing those awful pajamas. "I don't think that. I never thought that. I kissed you because I wanted to."

"Maybe out of gratitude," he suggested.

"Oh, for heaven's sake. Didn't anyone ever tell you you're a very attractive man? What about all those women who were lined up outside the house waiting in line to throw themselves at you after your wife left?"

"What are you talking about? Nobody's ever thrown themselves at me."

"That's not what I heard."

"I should never have taken you to town," he said with a frown.

"People talk," she agreed.

"What else did they say?"

"Um...well, are you sure you want to know?"

"Go ahead."

"That you're fair and honest and you never hire women."

"Until now."

"I appreciate your breaking your rules for me, Parker. I—I really like it here. I'd work for you for nothing. But...that's probably not a good idea. I feel at home here, maybe it's because I can't remember if I have a home or a family of my own. And if it will make you feel any better, I'll try to keep my hands off you. But you can't, you know, look at me the way you do. I'm not made of stone." Her voice shook just slightly as she came to the end of her sentence.

"I know," he said gruffly. He knew only too well what she was made of. His heart started to pound in his chest as he tried not to look at her the way he did, tried not to remember how she felt in his arms and how much he wanted her. "Well, I guess we understand each other a little better," he said. But did he? Did she? In any case she nodded and gave him a small smile. Then she raised one hand in a gesture that was clearly goodbye and, as gracefully as he could, he left the room.

Christine sat staring at the closed door, her body tired and aching, her mind in turmoil. She was so new to this game, she had no perspective, no plan, no frame of reference. She only knew that she wanted him, wanted him to make love to her, wanted to tear down the barriers between them, between him and the world.

She thought that tonight was a start, a kind of beginning. That there might be possibilities. That he... that she... But he'd made it clear she was wrong. It meant nothing to him. And everything to her. She sighed and put her amnesia book on the table next to her bed. Then she turned out the light. She was exhausted, physically and mentally. But thoughts of Parker, visions of his face, memories of his kisses, kept her awake long into the night. Even more than learning about her own past, she wanted to know about his. Sooner or later she'd find out. From someone. But she wished it could be from him.

Chapter Five

She was home. Sarah Robinson, with her hair flying in every direction, her long legs in blue jeans, arrived the next afternoon to spend the weekend. Christine stood at the kitchen window and watched, fascinated, as the girl ran like a graceful colt from the barn to the stable and then to the house. She burst into the kitchen and stopped short, out of breath, when she saw Christine.

"What smells so good?" she asked, poised in the doorway and eyeing Christine curiously.

"Spice cookies," Christine said, taking a pan out of the oven.

"Are you the new cook?" Sarah asked. "The one with amnesia?"

"How'd you guess?" Christine asked, pausing to stare into eyes the exact blue of her father's.

"I'm smart," she confessed. "But I wish I wasn't. Then I wouldn't have to go to the Academy. I could go to school in Clear Creek." She reached for a cookie and crammed it into her mouth.

Christine nodded. "I saw that school yesterday. The one in town."

"What did you think? Isn't it nice? Was there anything wrong with it?"

"I—I couldn't really tell, from the outside," Christine said.

"Do you know what it's like to go to school in Denver?" Sarah asked, pouring herself a glass of milk from the refrigerator.

"I don't think I do. What *is* it like?"

"Awful. Terrible. I hate it," she announced.

"Why?"

"Cuz it's in Denver. I want to be here. Do you like it here?"

Christine looked out the window at the sheep grazing in the pasture, at the mountains in the distance and the sun shining on a narrow ribbon of river that wound through the valley. "Yes, I do," she said. "Who wouldn't?"

"My mom didn't," Sarah said, straddling the kitchen chair.

"Really?" Christine held her breath. If Parker knew his daughter was talking to his cook about his ex-wife, he wouldn't like it. Not at all. She wanted the girl to continue, but she didn't want to make Parker angry.

"Nope. She left when I was little. I used to think it was me she didn't like."

Christine stared as the girl talked to her as if she'd known her all her life. Her eyes, her cheekbones, were so much like Parker's, her lack of inhibition, her forthright nature, so different.

"I'm sure she does like you," Christine said, pouring herself a cup of tea and sitting at the table. Who wouldn't like this uninhibited, carefree creature, all arms and legs, and untamed energy?

"She's forgotten about me," Sarah said with an unconcerned shrug. Then she tilted her head to one side. "What's it like to have amnesia?"

"Well, it's kind of weird," Christine answered slowly. "It's like part of you is missing."

"Maybe that's what my mom has. Maybe that's why she can't remember me. Not even my birthday."

Christine swallowed hard over a lump in her throat. Under her breezy grown-up exterior, there was a little girl inside who'd been hurt badly by her mother's desertion. "When *is* your birthday?" she asked.

"March fourteenth. When's yours?"

Christine shook her head. "I don't know. I don't even know how old I am."

"We could look at your teeth. That's how you tell with horses."

Christine let her jaw fall open and Sarah braced her arms on the table and leaned forward to peer into Christine's mouth. At that moment Parker walked in the back door.

"What's going on here?" he asked, riffling his daughter's hair. "Don't frighten the new cook. She's not used to being examined by a wild twelve-year-old. She's used to getting some respect around here."

Sarah jumped back from the table and grinned impudently at her father. "From who, you and the boys?"

"And Pop," Parker assured her.

"I was just trying to find out how old she is," Sarah explained.

"She's not a horse," he said as Christine looked back and forth from father to daughter with envy at their easy banter.

Sarah giggled. "I know that. I knew she was your cook from the first minute I walked in here and smelled those cookies. Here, try one." She picked up a warm, soft cookie and handed it to her father, then watched as he chewed it. "You didn't tell me she was so pretty," she chided her father. Sarah reached up and gingerly touched Christine's curls. "Or that her hair was soft as a baby lamb's."

"That's because I wash it with Lanolux, guaranteed to bring out the shine in your fleece," Christine explained.

Sarah's eyes widened in amazement. "That reminds me," she said, "I gotta feed my baby lamb." She gave a little skip and twirled out the door, slamming it behind her.

Christine sat down, suddenly exhausted by the little whirlwind. "What an amazing child," she said. "How do you keep up with her?"

"I don't even try."

"She has so much energy."

"Fortunately they know how to direct it at the school."

"Is that why she's there?"

"It's a fine school. She's a smart girl. But headstrong. Opinionated and stubborn, too."

"I wonder where she got those traits," Christine mused under her breath.

He chose to ignore her remark. "I suppose she told you she wants to come home," Parker said.

Christine hesitated. She didn't want to betray Sarah's confidence, and yet she had a feeling she wasn't the first person Sarah'd told about not liking her school.

"What *did* she say?" Parker asking, taking another cookie.

"Just that she likes it *here*."

"Because she has no idea what ranch life is really about. She comes home for the weekend. She sees the newborn lambs and she takes her horse out riding and has Pop eating out of her hand. What she doesn't see is the backbreaking work, the day-to-day grind."

Christine poured some more tea in her cup from the pot on the table. "You make it sound pretty grim and yet you seem to like it."

"Of course I like it. It's my life."

"Then why..."

"Don't you start, too. And don't encourage her in this ranch life business. It's not a life for a woman. It's boring and lonely. Women want change, excitement. I know what you're thinking. It sounds sexist. Well, I don't care. I know what I know. Sarah's meant for other things."

He took a cold beer from the refrigerator. Christine assumed the conversation was over so she went to the pantry for a bag of rice and a can of tomatoes but when she came back he was still there, leaning against the counter.

It had been two days since she'd returned from town with him. And she'd hardly spoken to anyone except Parker's father since. She didn't mind. She was just grateful to be there, doing what she was good at. And there had been no complaints about the food, either from the men or from Parker. His father was easy to talk to. Or rather, easy to listen to.

Christine didn't have any tales of her childhood to tell, but Emilio had plenty. Plenty of tales of Parker's childhood, too, which Christine found illuminating. His son had loved the land and the animals from the beginning, adopting orphaned sheep and hand-feeding them just as his daughter was doing now. It amazed her that Parker didn't empathize with his daughter's wishes, since they were so similar to his own. But what did she know about parenting anyway?

She tried to ignore Parker's presence in the kitchen as she chopped onions and bell peppers, but it wasn't easy. It was partly his size, partly his bearing, partly those penetrating eyes, always watching, always assessing her, the suppressed energy that made her aware of him. That made her wonder what he was going to say or do next. And then there was the memory of the last time they were in the kitchen together. He'd probably forgotten. She'd tried, but she couldn't. Probably because there wasn't much else in her memory. But the touch of his lips on hers, combined with the smell of leather and the hard contours of his chest pressed against her breasts kept coming back to puzzle and to haunt her. What made him do it? Just repressed physical desire. That was obviously it. It had been a long time, perhaps since his wife left. Who could blame him for taking advantage of the new cook? Who'd taken advantage of whom, anyway?

She turned the gas on under a large frying pan and poured olive oil into it. And still he stayed, sipping his beer slowly. She didn't look at him, she didn't need to to know that he was still watching her, studying her. What did he want? Why didn't he say something? Her hands shook just slightly as she scooped the vegetables off the counter and dumped them in the pan.

Oil spattered against Christine's shirt and she reached for the white apron hanging from a hook on the wall. With a spoon still in one hand she pulled the apron over her head with the other, then awkwardly tried to tie it behind her. Without thinking he set his beer down and crossed the room, pulling the sash around her waist and knotting it tightly. The scent of her hair, of her skin, filled his senses. He told himself to move away before he did something he'd be sorry for. Again. But he didn't. He let his hands rest on her hips, fighting the urge to pull her back against him, to bury his face in the silky softness of her hair. She was breathing hard. He was afraid he couldn't breathe at all. Afraid his heart had stopped beating.

"Thanks," she said breathlessly.

"For what?" he demanded.

She held perfectly still. "For everything. Tying my apron. Giving me a job." Her voice was a whisper.

He backed off. Physically and mentally. He went back to the counter and picked up his beer. She was grateful to him. That was all. That was the reason she'd kissed him the other night, the reason she accepted his coming on to her. He knew he was attractive to most women. He knew they liked him, invited him to dinner, offered to help him out. But this was not most women. This was one special woman. And once she got to know him, and know what ranch life was really like, she'd leave just the way Cheryl had.

"You don't have to keep thanking me," he said brusquely.

"And you don't have to keep saying you're sorry," she said, turning from the stove to look at him.

He raised his eyebrows in surprise. "Did I say..."

"You were going to."

"Maybe I was. Anyway it's my turn to thank you. For the great meals. The men have never been happier."

She nodded and turned back to the stove. He finished his beer and tossed the bottle in the trash, then walked out the back door.

After dinner in the bunkhouse Sarah helped Christine clear the table, then carefully rinsed the dishes while Christine loaded the dishwasher.

"I could be a big help to you," Sarah said, handing Christine a salad plate. "Like peeling potatoes, or pulling weeds from the kitchen garden." She paused significantly. "If I lived here."

"I'll bet you could," Christine answered. "But you don't. Maybe after you graduate. Or even in the summer."

"Will you be here then?" Sarah asked, pouring herself a glass of cold milk to wash down a cookie she'd just snitched from the cookie jar.

"I suppose not," Christine said, trying to sound casual when she felt hollow inside thinking of her uncertain future.

"Then I have to stay here now. I'll help you and you'll teach me to cook. That's something I can't learn at school."

"You mean they don't have home economics anymore?"

Sarah turned the corners of her mouth down. "Uhuh. They don't have anything practical at my school. If I lived here I could join 4-H, and raise my own goats."

"Goats? I haven't seen any goats around."

"Cuz there aren't any. But goats get along real well with sheep. What I want to do is—"

Parker came in at that moment and interrupted their conversation. "Don't you have homework to do?" he asked his daughter.

She wrinkled her nose. "A little. I can do it tomorrow."

He shook his head. "I thought we had a deal. You can come home for the weekend anytime, but you have to get your homework done and let me check it before you go out on your horse."

"It's poetry, Dad. I don't understand it and we've gotta write a paper on it."

"Poetry?" Christine asked. "Can I see it?"

"But we're not finished," Sarah protested, looking desperately around the clean kitchen for something more to do.

"Yes, we are. Go get your book."

Reluctantly Sarah left the room and they heard her drag her feet up the stairs to her room.

"See what I mean?" Parker asked with a wry smile.

"About her being determined? You didn't expect to have a weak-willed child who said, 'How high?' when you said jump, did you?"

He shook his head, and stared out the window. "I guess I expected a boy who'd take over for me. When I got a girl I thought my wife would teach her to be a lady. Instead she left."

Christine held her breath, rubbing her already dry hands with a dish towel. She never expected him to say anything about his wife.

"It must have been a...a shock," Christine said softly.

"A shock?" An old feeling of bitterness welled up in his throat and burned like acid. "You could say that."

He dragged his gaze back to her. "I don't normally talk about it. I don't know why I am now."

She was afraid to speak, afraid to say too much or too little. What she wanted to say was, "Go on, go ahead. It's not good to keep things bottled up for twelve years."

"Maybe," she said, running a hand through her short curls, "it's because I'm not a part of your life. I'm just a stranger who's fallen out of the sky from an alien spaceship and someday I'll go back to my planet and take your secrets with me."

"So you heard all that," he said, and poured himself a cup of coffee from the stove. "Do you remember anything else about that first night?" he asked, glancing up over the brim of the cup.

"Like your undressing me and giving me a bath?" she asked.

So she knew. With an effort, he deliberately made his face a blank. He couldn't let the memories of that night show from a telltale gleam in his eye or a smile on his face.

"I must have a been a pretty sight," she sighed.

"I really don't remember," he lied. The memory of that episode lingered, played havoc with his dreams. He couldn't deny he'd seen her, every gentle curve, every flat surface, every bump, every bruise.

"That's good," she said, absently filling the salt shaker. "The funny thing about this amnesia is that while I can't remember anything from before the accident, everything since is engraved on my consciousness. Probably because I have nothing else to think about. Everything seems so fresh, so new, as if I've never seen it before. The air outside, every blade of grass, the sun, the sky... Every feeling I have is so intense, every sensation . . . That's why I'm afraid I over-reacted the other night. When you kissed me and I kissed you back, it was as if . . ."

He clenched his teeth. "You don't have to explain."

"I want to."

"It's not necessary."

"I know that. I just don't want you to think I'm like all those other women."

"I don't." She was like no other woman. But he couldn't say that. She'd get the wrong idea. The idea that he was going to do something about it. What he was going to do was just the opposite. He was going to stay the hell out of the kitchen, and if he was in there, he was not going to tie her apron strings, eat her cookies or drink her coffee. He crossed the room and poured his coffee down the sink. There.

When he turned he saw Sarah quietly standing in the doorway, her bright eyes moving from him to Christine and back again. How long had she been there, how much had she heard?

"Have you got it?" Christine asked, clearing the kitchen table of her cookbooks and recipes. She motioned to a chair and Sarah plunked her books and binder on the table. They sat next to each other, forgetting Parker in their concentration on the work in front of them, the overhead light shining on Sarah's straight, fine, flyaway hair and on Christine's shiny short brown curls.

He saw his daughter open her book, he heard Christine say something about the poet, about the poem, but he didn't know what. His mind was a jumble of thoughts, of painful memories and of unrealized expectations. Life hadn't turned out the way he'd thought it would, he realized as he quietly walked behind them and out the back door. He'd expected a boy, he'd gotten a girl. A bright, energetic girl he wouldn't trade for anyone. But he'd also expected a wife who'd stand by his side, only he'd been betrayed instead.

Christine, whose senses had just come alive, didn't know who she was or even who he was. It was best that she didn't. Because to know him meant to leave him. That's what he had to conclude when Cheryl left. He didn't know what else to think. Before she left he thought everything was fine. He thought he was in love. Thought she loved him back. Yes, it was a shock. A shock he thought he was over by now. Maybe he was. Maybe it was just the hurt that was still there.

He walked around in the dark, circling the barn, the pens, the sheds. Listened to the sound of crickets, to the blare of the TV from the bunkhouse and the laughter. Then he walked by the kitchen again, peered in the window. They were still there, Christine talking earnestly, Sarah listening intently, a frown puckering her forehead. It was a touching scene, but a twinge of anxiety hit him below the ribs. What was happening? Where was it all leading?

After breakfast the next morning, Christine went to the garden at the back of the house to dig root vegetables for a soup. The air was cool but the sun shone on the feathery carrot tops that poked through the rich soil. She was on her knees with a trowel in her hands when Parker found her.

"She's at it again," he said, dispensing with any kind of greeting.

Christine rocked backward. "What?"

"Sarah. She says you can teach her what she doesn't learn at the school in town. She's got it all figured out."

Standing above her and frowning at her the way he was doing was intimidating. "What did you say to her yesterday?" he continued.

"I don't know. Nothing. I certainly didn't encourage her. Although..."

"Although what?"

"I told her that if she did live at home and go to the school in town, I'd be happy to help her in any way I could."

"Even if you were permanent, it wouldn't work. You know why."

She sat squarely on the ground, her head tilted back to look up into his cool, clear blue eyes. "The ranch is no place for a woman or a girl, is that it?"

"I take it you don't agree with me."

"So far it suits me fine," she said mildly, "and Sarah..."

"So far," he repeated. "You haven't even been here two weeks and you're an expert at women and ranch life."

"I didn't say that." She felt the blood go to her head in an angry rush. "I just wonder how you would have liked being sent off to school in Denver at that age when you loved this place so much. I know, I know," she said seeing he was ready to dispute her, "you're a man, she's a girl. But don't you see how much alike you are?"

"Not really," he said dryly.

At that moment Sarah came trotting up on her mare Sugar and stopped at the edge of the fence. "Come riding with me," she called to them. It was not a request, it was an order. Christine smothered a smile. How could Parker not see the similarity between him and his daughter?

Christine looked at Parker and he looked at her. "Go ahead," she said.

"I think she means you," he said.

"Both of you," she shouted, reaching down to pat Sugar on the shoulder.

"I don't think I know how..." Christine said.

"Then it's time you learned," Parker said, extending his arm and pulling her up off the ground. She ended up facing him from inches away, his rough, calloused hand still holding hers, his eyes, the color of the Colorado sky, locked on hers. For one crazy moment she almost thought he was going to kiss her. And for one crazy moment she wanted him to. More than anything. But Sarah's voice cut through the suddenly heavy atmosphere.

"Hey, you guys," she yelled. And they broke apart. Christine brushed the dirt off her hands, feeling as guilty as a teenager caught by her parents instead of his daughter. The next thing she knew she was outside the barn door, mounting a friendly, aged mare called Cindy.

"Foot through the stirrup front to back," Sarah instructed, still astride her horse.

"Now swing up," Parker said, giving her a boost and letting his hand linger on her fanny just a moment longer than absolutely necessary. What was wrong with him? What was it about her he couldn't resist? Those smoky gray eyes that changed with her mood? The touch of her hand, the sweet curve of her hip? It was all of the above and more. It was her smile, the one she tried to hide. It was the way she looked at him when she thought he wasn't looking. With something that might have been desire. He didn't know. It had been so long.

What was he doing, giving riding lessons to the cook when he had office work to do today, bills to pay and calls to make to order new breeding stock? Maybe it was just too nice a day to stay inside. Maybe it had been too long since he'd gone for a ride with his daughter just for pleasure.

"Keep a firm grip on the front of the saddle," he instructed Christine. "Now, take the reins and hold them loosely."

She did as he said, then glanced at him. "What next?"

"Just stay there. I'll go saddle up Chance."

Sarah clapped her hands and her horse pawed the ground. "I can't believe he's coming with us," she said to Christine.

He went back into the barn to get the Appaloosa, wishing Sarah wouldn't make such a big deal of it. Christine might think he was going with them to be with her, when it was just the day, the season, spring in the air. Whatever it was, it felt good to be throwing a saddle on Chance, to hear his welcoming whinny. "Try to act casual," he muttered in the horse's ear. "Like we do this every day." He should do it every day, he thought as he joined the others and mounted his favorite horse.

Sarah was telling Christine what to do. "Keep your arms straight and don't twist the reins," she said.

"Ready?" her father asked, noting with pride his daughter's erect posture, her ease and comfort on her spirited mount. She was an accomplished rider. She should be. She'd been riding since she could walk. Pop had seen to that.

Christine's forehead was etched with tiny worry lines. He reached over and untwisted her reins. Then he put his hand on her shoulder for reassurance. "To start going, press your legs against the side of the horse. Don't worry, she hates to run. A real wimp."

"Just like me," Christine said under her breath.

"I don't believe that," he said more to himself than to her as they left the corral, three abreast. "No wimp would have taken this job. No wimp would live through being struck by lightning."

She shrugged, but a flush of pleasure tinted her cheeks.

Sarah glanced at Christine who was clutching the reins tightly in her hands and she smiled delightedly. "She's doing good, Dad, isn't she?" she asked.

"Not bad."

"Can we go a little faster?" Sarah asked, trotting ahead of the others. "I'll meet you guys at the duck pond." Without waiting for an answer she galloped off.

"I thought you were supposed to go riding *with* her," Christine said. "I'm spoiling your ride. Your quality time together. That wasn't the idea."

Parker watched his daughter disappear in a cloud of dust over the rise. What was the idea? Had the little imp done this deliberately to throw him together with Christine? Sarah had had nothing but good words for the cook since she'd seen her. He knew it was partly because she sensed a potential ally in her struggle to stay on the ranch. But could she also have something else in mind? A replacement mother? After knowing her for only one day? Ridiculous.

"Let's try trotting," he suggested, shifting the reins to one hand and nudging his horse with one knee.

Christine's eyes widened, and she gripped the horse tightly with her legs as Cindy increased her speed, lifting the front leg on one side of its body along with the hind leg on the other side. The two legs hit the ground at the same time and they were riding together, the two horses and the two people, only a foot apart. The wind blew their hair, the horses' manes. Instead of bouncing helplessly in her saddle, Christine rose and fell with the rhythm of the horse.

"Hey," he said, "what are you doing?"

"I don't know," she shouted into the wind. "Am I doing it right?" Without waiting for his answer, she laughed delightedly and pushed old Cindy to a gallop. Parker followed, watching the wind toss her hair, mold her shirt to her body, wondering for the hundredth time what she'd been in her other life. Who'd taught her to cook, who'd taught her to ride and, more important, who'd taught her to kiss? For some reason he wished it had been him.

Chapter Six

Parker dug his heels into his horse's flank and galloped after Christine, feeling the wind in his face, and the power of the horse under him. When he caught up with her she flashed him a triumphant smile. They rode together into the wind. He couldn't remember the last time he'd ridden for pleasure. Just for the hell of it. Couldn't remember when he'd ridden with someone. For pleasure. And it was pleasure. A pleasure to watch her ride high in the saddle, back straight. The sun shone on her fawn-colored curls. Her smile dazzled him. He couldn't tear his eyes from her.

At the duck pond he dismounted and reached for her. She swung around and slid into his arms. Her knees buckled and he caught her. He slanted a kiss across her lips. There was a moment of hushed silence as if he'd taken her by surprise. Maybe he had. But when she shivered in his arms, he heated things up. One hot, hungry kiss, but it wasn't enough. He felt her hands tighten on his shoulders and when her lips parted, his tongue caressed hers. Hungry for more, he claimed her for a deep, soul-searching kiss. She sighed and he pulled her closer, tighter. The wind died down to a whisper. The only sound was her breathing—or was it his—hard and fast.

She pulled away and braced her hands on his arms. "That was... that was wonderful," she breathed, her gray eyes cloudy, her lips so full, so desirable he leaned forward, wondering....

"The ride...or the kiss?" he asked. He knew, he just had to hear her say it.

"Both."

It was all the encouragement he needed. His arms went around her and crushed her to him. Forgotten were all the words of warning he'd given himself, the pain and the anguish of the past, the proximity of his daughter. All he could think about was Christine and how much he wanted her. He cupped her face in his hands, studied her long-lashed eyes, straight nose and determined chin... angled his mouth to taste again, to sample....

The pounding of his heart seemed to reverberate until the ground shook under his feet. Like a stampede coming their way.

"Hey," Sarah shouted, reining her horse on the other side of the pond. "What's going on?"

They jumped apart as if the earth had parted beneath them. Would it do any good to say "nothing"? As calmly as he could he led his horse to the pond to drink. "What took you so long?" he asked Sarah as she approached.

"I took a little detour," Sarah explained. "So I didn't have to wait for you slowpokes." She grinned and he shook his head and grinned back at her.

"How'd she do?" Sarah asked her father, nodding at Christine.

"Fine. She's a natural. I guess she's had experience somewhere along the line."

Christine sauntered up to join them. "That was fun," she said.

"You looked like you were enjoying it," Sarah said with another of her broad knowing smiles.

The kid was too smart for her own good, Parker thought. And too cheeky.

"We'll have to find her something more her speed, won't we, Dad?" she asked.

He caught Christine's gaze and he felt the heat rise through his body. With just a look, she had the power to arouse him. Power he'd vowed he never let any woman have again. Without answering, he got back on his horse as Christine was telling Sarah she thought Cindy was good enough for her.

"I'd better get back," he said with a glance at the two of them standing there together, wind-blown, red-cheeked, with the pond and the blue sky behind them. He had to escape. From Christine, from Sarah, from all this togetherness, before he forgot this wasn't real life. Real life was hard work, and if he hung around much longer having fun he'd want more, and he'd want it to last. And that wasn't going to happen.

"Do you like Christine?" Sarah asked her father after the men had cleared out of the dining room that evening and he was finishing his coffee.

He set his cup down. "Of course I like her. Why?"

"Cuz she likes you."

"Does she?" He glanced at his daughter. "How do you know?"

She grinned over her second helping of chocolate pudding. "She told me. And I can just tell anyway." She paused and licked her spoon. "Are you surprised?"

"No. I mean yes. What I mean is adults use the word 'like' in a different way than kids do. I wouldn't hire someone I didn't like, and I'm sure Christine wouldn't work for someone she didn't 'like.'"

"She might. I mean she had nowhere to go and no choice. She doesn't know who she is. She doesn't even know if she's ever been in love before." Sarah's eyes were wide with wonder.

He frowned. "It sounds like you've been asking her a lot of questions. I hope you're not making a pest of yourself. She's been through a lot you know."

"I know, she told me. She's a good cook, isn't she?"

"Very good."

"Don't you think I should learn to cook?"

"Sure. Someday."

"What about now? If I lived here, she'd teach me to cook and help me with my homework, like today. What if we found out she was a teacher in her real life, then would you let me stay here?"

"No."

"What if she was a psychiatrist and she told you I had to stay here or I'd have a nervous breakdown, then could I stay?"

"Sweetheart . . ."

"What if . . ."

"No. You're staying at the Academy. Look, it's almost summer vacation."

"In the fall then, can I stay here and go to school in Clear Creek?"

"Sarah!" The girl never stopped pushing him to his limits.

"Okay," she said, completely undaunted. Then she left the room, balancing a glass, her empty bowl and a large serving dish. He was certain he hadn't heard the end of it.

He left the dining room and walked through the house. The living room door was open and he walked in. It was cool and smelled slightly musty. They hadn't used the room for months, maybe years. When he was first married, Cheryl changed the furniture around, added a reclining chair, recovered the couch. When she left, he closed the door on the room like he'd closed off the part of his heart that had to do with love. And he had no desire to reopen either one.

But Sarah was dragging a dusty card table out of the closet. When she turned and saw him she smiled delightedly as if he'd never yelled at her, as if she had no doubt she'd eventually get her way, just by chipping away at his resistance. The way she'd done when she wanted to raise baby chicks when she was five. But she wouldn't. This was different. This was important. This was her future.

"Oh, good, just in time to play Pictionary with us," she said, leaning the table against the wall.

He backed toward the door. "Not tonight."

"You have to. We need an even number for teams. So far we just have me and Christine and Pop."

"I have work to do," he said firmly.

"Then could you just make a fire for us in the fireplace?" she asked with a little shiver to illustrate her request and he nodded. Just as long as he didn't get roped into some game. Just as long as he didn't have to spend the evening in the same room as Christine, watching her smile curve the corners of her mouth, her gray eyes change color to match her mood, hear her voice with a hint of husky sensuality she wasn't even aware of. No, he was definitely busy tonight. Doing something. Anything. He lit the paper under the kindling and turned to tell Sarah once again he wasn't playing, but she was gone, the card table on end where she'd left it.

Christine came into the room wearing a pair of soft, prewashed jeans, a lambswool sweater and thick slippers he'd loaned her when she was sick. She had a way of taking his breath away when he least expected it. When he least expected her. Even when he did expect her. Which made it difficult for him to speak, to know what to say. Especially after what happened that afternoon. The memory of their kisses, the heat of their passion, hovered in the air between them.

She seemed to have the same problem catching her breath. Her eyes darted to the fire, then to him and for a long moment she stood hesitantly in the doorway staring at him. "I wasn't...I didn't think...Sarah said we were going to play a game."

"You are," he said, picking up the brass poker and nudging the log. "I'm just making the fire. Don't worry, I'm not staying."

"I'm not worried," she said with deliberate calm, walking toward the fire and stretching her hands out in front of her. "Why *don't* you stay? Sarah would like that."

"Would *you?*" he asked impulsively. What made him say that? What could she possibly say without being rude?

"I, uh, of course I would. But that's not the point. The point is for you to spend time with your daughter. Besides, she says you need four for Pictionary. She's gone to get your father."

"I don't believe my father's playing Pictionary," he said. "The last time my father stayed up past eight o'clock was when two pregnant ewes gave birth to twins in the same evening four years ago."

"Do *you* know how to play Pictionary?" he asked, taking four folding chairs out of the closet.

She stared at the wall, her mind a blank. "I don't know. Maybe it will come back to me. I never know what I know how to do until I try it."

"Like horseback riding . . . or kissing."

She studied the pattern in the hand-woven carpet. "Yes."

"Those came back to you."

"Or maybe you're just a good teacher."

"Or maybe you've had a lot of practice."

"Riding?"

"Kissing."

She glanced up, trying to read the expression in his eyes. Was Parker Robinson teasing her or did he seriously want to know? "Does it matter?" she asked.

"Aren't you curious about your background?" he countered.

"Sometimes," she admitted. "And other times I don't want to know. As if I've been cut loose and allowed to be or do whatever I want. It's . . . liberating."

Voices in the hall prevented him from answering. Sarah had her grandfather by the hand and was pulling him into the living room. "We need you, Grandpa," she said. "So we can have two on each team." She set the game on the table and looked around the room at the fire now burning brightly in the fireplace and at her father and Christine. Before anyone could protest she had them sitting around the table with a stack of cards in the middle and a pad of drawing paper and pencils.

"You're Christine's partner," she said to her father, easing Parker into a folding chair with her hand on his shoulder.

"Here's what you do," Sarah explained eagerly, one knee on her chair, the other foot on the floor. "When you get your assignment, you try to draw it so your partner will know what it's supposed to be."

Her grandfather nodded slowly and picked up a pencil in his gnarled hands. Sarah plunked an egg timer in the middle of the table. "We each get three minutes to guess. Should I go first?" she asked quickly before anyone could protest or quit before they'd begun.

Christine looked at Parker who'd opened his mouth to say something to his daughter, but closed it when she didn't give him a chance. In a flash Sarah had read her card and drawn a picture. Her grandfather looked at it over his glasses and his eyebrows knit together in concentration.

"Is it a flower?" he asked.

"No, no, no." Sarah shook her head with frustration.

"I don't think you're allowed to talk, are you?" Christine inquired mildly.

"Sorry," Sarah said, pressing her fingers against her mouth.

"So you have played this before," Parker said in a low tone.

Christine met his gaze across the table, but she had no answer. Had she played it? With who? Children? Whose children?

Sarah drew more pictures and her grandfather dutifully guessed, but never got it right. The answer was windmill. Then it was Christine's turn. She selected a card that said "Royal Wedding." She sketched a head with a crown and showed it to Parker. He shrugged.

"Come on, Dad, try," Sarah urged.

"A hat," he said.

Christine shook her head and drew a church and a steeple. She drew stick figures of a man and woman. The man wore a top hat and the woman wore a long dress with a train and a crown on her head. Parker guessed church, then stopped. Sarah squirmed in her chair hardly able to keep from shouting out the answer.

"A wedding," he said reluctantly.

"You're good at drawing," Sarah said, studying the picture of the bride and groom. "Isn't she, Dad?"

Without looking at the drawing, he nodded.

"I could sure learn a lot from Christine if I lived here," she said.

"I'm sure you could," he said with surprising mellowness.

"And I could raise goats."

"I think we've already been through this a few times," Parker said. "This is a sheep ranch, you know."

"Goats browse where it's not good enough for sheep," Sarah informed everyone at the table. "They can clear the land of brush for you," she said with a smug smile.

"That may be true," her grandfather said. "But goats need just as much care as sheep."

"That's why I need to be here," she said, her eyes glowing. "All the time. To take care of my goats."

"Sarah," her father said, "I thought we were playing a game. You can't raise goats because you're not here all the time. You go to school in Denver," he said with surprising patience, "and after school you'll go to college. In the summer you can come home. You can have a pet, a dog or a cat, but..."

"A dog or a cat?" Her voice rose as the impact of his words hit. "I don't want a pet. I want goats. A whole herd of goats and if you don't get them for me, I'll get them for myself." With that she stalked out of the room, head held high, shoulders back. The room was silent except for the hiss of the logs in the fireplace.

The old man braced his arm on the table and rose slowly. "Got ideas of her own, that girl," he said. "Don't know where she gets 'em." He shuffled to the door then turned to look at Parker. "The back forty might do for goats," he suggested.

Parker took a deep breath. "You're not taking her side, are you?" he asked.

"Just an idea," he said. "If she was a boy..."

"But she's not. She's a girl. An intelligent girl with a stubborn streak. And a few crazy ideas. She'll get over them."

Emilio nodded and left the room. But the tension remained. Parker stood and paced back and forth in front of the fireplace. Christine took her drawing of the church and the bride and groom and put it in her pocket.

"I suppose you're on her side, too," Parker said with a glance at Christine still sitting at the table staring off into space.

"Hmm?" She pulled herself out of her reverie. "I can understand why she loves it here and wants to stay," she said.

"You can?"

"So can you," she said. "And don't tell me it's because you're a man. Women can appreciate beauty, solitude, fresh air...."

"I know that. I'm not a complete sexist."

He sat in the chair next to the fireplace, stretched his legs out in front of him and stared into the flames. His forehead was creased with lines she wanted to smooth. Despite her siding with Sarah in this argument, she understood his frustration with the girl. But not his insistence on her staying at boarding school. She realized it had something to do with his ex-wife. Probably everything had something to do with her. She cast a long shadow over his and his daughter's life. And after today Christine felt herself falling helplessly under the same shadow.

Christine touched the drawing she'd made, smoothing the paper between her fingers. She had no trouble drawing a picture of a bride and groom or a church. She knew exactly how the veil swept past the waist, how it felt fastened to the headpiece. She could almost hear the music in the church. Smell the flowers. Her stomach knotted and she felt like she was going to faint. Instinctively she put her head between her knees.

"What's wrong?" Parker got to his feet and crossed the floor in two strides.

"Nothing. I..." She looked up and the blood came rushing back to her head. "I had a feeling, a memory... and now it's gone." She swallowed hard, trying to repress the memory, but why?

"Something from the past?" he asked, his brow furrowed with concern.

She drew a ragged breath. "Maybe. I don't know." She tried to stand. He pulled her up with strong hands and she stood there for a long moment, her eyes filled with longing for what she couldn't have until she broke away.

"She likes you, too. Part of it is, I don't want her to get too attached to you."

"For fear I'll leave."

"You *will* leave," he said.

"Yes." She knew she'd have to leave. Had to find out who she was and where she belonged. Because she had to know, and because there was no place for her here, not permanently.

She turned on the heel of her slipper before he could see the tears welling in her eyes.

"Wait a minute," he said.

But she walked out the door, down the hall and into her room. Not her room. His den. Nothing here was hers. Not even her clothes. Soon she would leave here, before it was too late. Before she'd fallen in love with this place and with its owner.

The next afternoon Parker found Christine in the henhouse gathering eggs. "Can I talk to you?" he asked from the doorway.

She slid the basket of eggs over her arm and stepped outside. The soft sound of hens clucking filled the spring air. Parker stared off into the hills in the distance and she wondered if he'd forgotten why he'd come. She studied his profile, his strong nose, stubborn chin and broad forehead. Finally he turned toward her, his forehead creased with lines.

"I had a call from the employment office."

Her heart fell. Her throat clogged with sadness. She knew what was coming. She was going to be fired. She'd been expecting it, but that didn't make it any easier. She hated to leave this place, this safe haven. Most of all, she hated to leave Parker. But she held her chin high and looked him in the eye. "Did they find someone for you?"

"Yes. A man with some experience who doesn't mind the isolation. At least that's what they tell me. He can't start for another week though. So I was wondering..."

"Of course. I'll be glad to stay until he comes." Christine was proud of her steady voice.

The lines in his forehead disappeared. He thought she'd fall apart. Well, he didn't know her. Nobody knew her. Least of all herself.

"Thanks," he said, then he turned and left.

Somehow she got through the day. She made vegetable soup for lunch with Sarah's help. The girl chopped carrots and celery while Christine made a meat loaf for dinner.

After dinner Sarah dragged out old home videos and then went to Christine's room to drag her to the living room to watch them.

"It's my last night, you know," Sarah said. "I won't be back for two weeks, cuz next week is my class ski trip."

"I—I won't be here then. Did you hear? Your dad found a real cook."

Sarah's face fell. "What?"

"So the next time I see you will be in Denver," Christine continued cheerfully. "Because it's time for me to go find out who I am."

"I know who you are," Sarah insisted. "You're... Christine, don't go," she pleaded. Her eyes filled with tears and Christine blinked back a few of her own. She hugged the girl tightly and promised to come and see her. They wiped their eyes on Christine's tissues and Christine gave in to her request to watch the videos with her.

To her surprise Parker and his father were in the living room waiting for them. The tape was cued up and a fire was blazing in the fireplace.

The videotape showed a laughing, skinny little girl on her pony riding around the corral with her father holding the bridle. There was her grandfather holding a baby lamb, the ranch hands cavorting in the background and maybe even a former cook or two in a tall white hat. But there was no sign of Sarah's mother. Of course not. What did she expect? Parker looked younger, but not much happier. Out of the corner of her eye she watched him watching himself and his family with a nostalgic smile on his face. Did he know how lucky he was to have this family? Probably.

After they'd watched the tape, Christine and Sarah made popcorn and the four of them ate it together in the living room. For a going-away party, it wasn't bad at all.

When Sarah left the next day, she hugged Christine tightly and made her promise to visit her at school. Then she jumped into her father's truck and they drove to Clear Creek to meet a friend whose parents were driving the two girls back to Denver. The same Clear Creek where Christine was supposed to have taken the bus from that day so long ago, and yet such a short time ago. Soon she'd go back there, get on the bus this time for sure. No more stalling, she thought as she returned to an empty kitchen.

It wasn't empty for long. Parker's father Emilio came in for a cup of coffee and sat down at the kitchen table. "Hear you'll be leaving us," he said.

Christine glanced up from the old cookbook she was thumbing through. "Yes," she said. "You'll be getting a real cook."

"You're about as real as they come, to my mind," he said, studying her under his bushy eyebrows.

"Thank you, but... I'm not making any progress here."

"It's that son of mine," he grumbled.

"Oh, no. I mean in recovering my memory."

"Humph," he said as if he didn't believe her.

"Parker has been great, really. Giving me the job and everything."

"Needs a wife."

"Yes, maybe. But I don't think he wants one."

"Doesn't know what he wants."

Christine couldn't help but smile despite the sadness that crept into her heart. The idea of Parker not knowing what he wanted was almost funny.

"I know what I want," the old man continued. "A grandson to leave the place to."

"What about Sarah?"

"She'll marry somebody. Move away."

"I don't know about that," Christine said. "She loves this place."

He shook his head.

"Don't give up," she urged him.

"I won't if you won't," he said with a sudden smile.

She returned his smile, but she'd already given up. Given up hoping she'd ever be back there, ever break through Parker's defenses, ever find love, real love. Because despite her loss of memory, somehow she knew one thing. And that was that true love is a rare and precious thing, and that if you're lucky enough to find it, you should never let it go.

Chapter Seven

For the next week Christine studiously avoided Parker. It wasn't really hard because it was clear he was avoiding her. She cooked, and in between cooking she gardened, she rode old Cindy to the duck pond and back and tried not to think about the future. The future without Parker, without the ranch. Instead she memorized the view from the front porch, of green pastures and purple mountains in the distance. Of grazing sheep and cloudless skies. She inhaled great gulps of fresh mountain air and vowed never to forget this interlude in her life no matter what lay ahead of her. Or what happened before she came there.

It was easy to be philosophical during the day when she was busy. But at night after she'd loaded the dishwasher and hung the cast-iron skillets and copper-bottomed saucepans back on the rack in the kitchen, it was a different matter. She went to her room and tried not to ask herself what if. What if she went to the Department of Missing Persons and nobody was missing her? What if she wandered around looking for herself and never found a clue as to who she was? What if she couldn't get on the bus again and simply wandered around Clear Creek? What if she never saw Parker again, never saw Sarah, either? Never returned to see the ranch under a warm summer sun, with the lambs frolicking on the new grass, and never saw it under a blanket of fresh snow?

When the new cook came she allowed herself two days to show him around, from the kitchen to the bunkhouse to the garden. But by the second day he was whipping up a huge batch of chili and a pan of corn-bread with one hand and a mountain of tapioca with the other and she realized with a pang she wasn't needed there anymore. After dinner she swallowed her pride and asked Parker for a ride to town the next day. He said sure, and disappeared into his office.

She knew he was relieved to have her go. She saw it in his eyes, heard it in his voice. There was no need to say any more. So when he knocked on the door to her room later that evening she was surprised. He stepped inside and looked around. She hoped he was pleased to see she'd left it exactly the way she'd found it by removing the vase of wildflowers, folding away the colorful af-ghan and packing her clothes in a small bag Parker had loaned her the last time she'd tried to leave. Or maybe he didn't notice.

He noticed. Parker felt a growing emptiness in the house and she wasn't even gone yet. He also felt guilty at forcing her to leave. Guilty and worried. He was worried she'd wander around Denver not knowing where to go or what to do. The same worries he'd had the last time she'd tried to leave. Only worse. Last time he barely knew her, this time he'd grown accustomed to having her around. Gotten used to seeing her in the kitchen when he walked by the window. To eating her gourmet food, hearing her talk with his father, or rather *listen* to him, watching her ride through the pasture when he was mending fences. It was strange how well she fit in. Maybe it was because she didn't know where she was supposed to fit in. Anyway, this time he was taking no chances on her not getting on the bus. He was driving her all the way to Denver. He had a good excuse, too.

"I can give you a ride into Denver tomorrow," he said abruptly, finally dragging his eyes from the empty bureau, from the wood paneling, to look at her.

"What?"

"I'm meeting some other purebred breeders there. Hope to sell them some of my rams and maybe pick up something. I'm looking for a couple of ewes to improve my stock."

She sat on the edge of her bed and looked at him, her eyes wide with surprise. "You mean you're taking the rams with you?" she asked.

He shook his head. "Just pictures and specs. No rams allowed in the hotel."

"Hotel?" she repeated.

"I'm staying a few days. Naturally I'll stop in and see Sarah. Then I have to go to the meeting of the Colorado Sheepbreeders Association. Actually I was asked to give a talk on heredity and environment."

She stared at him with her mouth open.

"What's wrong?" he asked, crossing his arms over his chest. "Is it so surprising that I can talk about sheep? Most people are surprised I can talk about anything else."

"No, but . . . you never said anything."

"I haven't seen you," he explained. Then he paused. He'd seen her. Seen her on the horse, seen her in the dining room and in the garden. Seen her everywhere, but didn't let on. He knew she was avoiding him as he was avoiding her. "And I didn't know if I could get away until now. But lambing is going well and Pop seems to have more energy, so I thought, why not?"

Why not? Because it meant spending hours in the car with Christine. Taking a chance that if he saw her in Denver, after she'd found out who she was, he'd feel better.

She was still looking at him, her eyes narrowed, skepticism showing in the tilt of her head. Maybe he hadn't explained it very well. Maybe he'd made it sound like too much of a coincidence. His going to Denver the same day she was. Maybe it was.

"I thought we'd leave first thing in the morning," he said off handedly to Christine. "It's about a five-hour drive."

She drew a quick, sharp breath. Did she wonder as he did how they'd fill the hours? What they'd talk about? What they'd do when they got there? He did. "I assumed you had no place to stay so I made a reservation for you at the hotel," he said. "It'll be filled with sheep breeders but they're usually not too loud and obnoxious."

"I guess I ought to thank you for all this," she said, her eyebrows scrunched together, "but—"

"Don't bother." He cut her off, afraid she'd object. "It's no trouble since I'm going anyway." Then he said good-night, turned on his heel and left her room.

The next morning Christine said goodbye to Emilio for the second time. This time she felt the finality of the situation somewhere in the pit of her stomach and it took an effort to hold her tears in check. She felt a little foolish when Parker's father just smiled and patted her cheek as if he knew she'd be back. Then she walked out the front door, staring straight ahead, her bag in her hand, and got into Parker's car. He threw his overnight bag in the trunk along with hers and they left the ranch.

It was like the last time he'd driven her into Clear Creek and yet it wasn't. The miles flew by as the scenery changed from pasture to high desert. Occasionally she glanced at Parker, noticing the way his crisp blue-and-white striped shirt fit on his broad shoulders, how it contrasted with his suntanned skin, realizing she'd never seen him in anything but denim. He kept his eyes on the road.

She wondered what he was thinking about as he drove. Maybe he was rehearsing his speech in his mind while she sat there admiring the way his city clothes fit his hard, well-muscled rancher's body. She knew she shouldn't even glance his way, but anything was better than sitting there trying to remember her past. Whatever he was thinking about, he obviously preferred it to talking to her.

When they'd crossed the last mountain pass and descended into the urban sprawl that was the outskirts of Denver, she felt her heart rate increase. She stared out the passenger window as if some familiar sight might suddenly appear and her memory would open like a closed door. But it didn't. She sighed.

"What's wrong?" he asked, navigating the city streets as competently as he rode through a herd of sheep on his horse.

"Nothing. Everything." She pressed her hand against her forehead. "I have this feeling of impending doom. As if I'm about to find out I'm an ax murderer."

He nodded. "Maybe you escaped from one of those work crews out on the highway."

"And I stumbled onto your pasture with my tent and my diamond necklace after sawing the chain off my foot."

He shot her an amused glance. "Should we stop at the post office and have a look at the Wanted posters?"

She shivered. "No thanks. I guess I'll go straight to the central police station and register with the missing persons like they told me to."

"You're not going today, are you?"

It was three o'clock by the dashboard digital clock. They were in the middle of a traffic jam in a strange city, surrounded by high-rise buildings and concrete everywhere. "I should, but I don't want to. I want to postpone it as long as I can. What's wrong with me?" she asked helplessly. How should Parker know what was wrong with her?

"You're scared," he said. "Scared of the unknown. That's normal." He pulled into the hotel parking lot.

Being scared might be normal, but was it normal to be checking into a downtown hotel dressed like a cowgirl? Was it normal to feel all quivery inside like a bowl of jelly when hearing from the room clerk that her room connected to his? When Parker placed the key into her palm and folded her fingers around it, her pulse jumped wildly. The key made an imprint on her skin she thought might never go away. She didn't know why she couldn't just pull her hand away, say thank you and go up to her room, but she could only stand there locked in his sky-blue gaze. The voices in the lobby faded away, the ringing telephones, bellboys carrying luggage all disappeared. It was just the two of them. Until a tall man in a Stetson hat slapped Parker on the back. And Christine pulled her hand back and stuffed it into her pocket.

"Heard you were coming," the man said to Parker. "'Bout time you showed at one of these things." His gaze swung from Parker to Christine, and he rocked back on the heels of his hand-tooled leather boots. "Wait a minute. Who might this be?"

Good question, Christine thought. Just what she wanted to know. Parker handled it smoothly. "Just a friend I gave a ride to town. Christine, meet Mike Adams."

Christine shook the broad hand he extended. Just a friend, she reminded herself. That's all you are.

"She'll be joining us at the dinner tonight, then. Got an extra place at the table."

"Oh, I don't think..." Christine protested with a glance at Parker.

"Don't think it will be interesting? With Parker here talking about heredity and environment? Watch out or you'll hurt his feelings," Mike Adams admonished with a wag of his finger in her direction.

She smiled weakly and followed Parker to the elevator. When they reached the fourth floor and were standing next to each other at their respective doors, she paused with the key in her hand.

"It won't really hurt your feelings if I don't go to the dinner, will it?"

"Of course not. It would be boring."

"I can't believe that. I'm sure it will be very interesting. But the thing is I don't have anything to wear to something like that.'' She looked down at her wrinkled jeans.

"I understand," he said curtly, turned the key in the lock and walked into his room, closing the door behind him.

Christine stood staring at the closed door. Had she hurt his feelings? Did Parker Robinson, the tough rancher, have feelings to hurt? After all he'd done for her it was the last thing she'd want to do. Slowly she opened the door to her room. There was a huge bed covered in a floral spread in mauve and pink. At the window, drapes to match. And a sitting area with a table and two chairs. She looked into the bathroom, which was done in black and white. A pile of fluffy towels were stacked next to the extra-long tub. She sighed at the sudden luxury.

Then she went back and stared at the connecting door. There was no sound from his room. Suddenly she felt more alone than ever before in her short memory. Which wasn't saying much, but it still sent a chill up her spine. Steeling her courage, she knocked on the door to Parker's room.

He opened it, his shirt unbuttoned halfway to his waist. Her eyes locked onto the broad expanse of chest, the dark hair that curled lightly over his skin, and she lost her voice, her nerve and her composure all at once.

"Yes?"

She cleared her throat. "I was wondering," she said, finally finding her vocal cords. "If I could borrow some more money. Then I could go downstairs and buy something to wear and come to the dinner." He didn't say anything. He must not want her to come, but now it was too late to back off. "I mean, if you think it would be okay. I mean if it's all right, I'd like to hear your speech, but if not . . .'' Oh, why did he have to be so noncommittal, so unemotional. Couldn't he just give her a clue as to what he wanted her to do? But he didn't. Not Parker. He pulled out his wallet, extracted a credit card and handed it to her.

"Thanks," she said. And closed the door between them before he could.

In the lobby there were several shops. The saleswoman was almost as helpful as the lady who'd helped her buy her jeans in Clear Creek. She didn't have a large selection, but what she had was elegant and classy. Perhaps too classy for sheepbreeders, but after days of blue jeans, Christine was ready for something black with thin straps, cut low in the back. She had no idea how she'd pay Parker back for the extravagance of this dress along with the shoes and stockings and underwear to go with it, but somehow she'd do it.

She smiled to herself as she rode up in the elevator with the shopping bag in her hand. How long had it been since she'd had a new dress and someplace to wear it? Had it only been weeks, or perhaps years? She must have worn the diamond necklace to something, with someone. But where and with whom?

Back in her room, she hung her new dress on a hanger and ran a bath in the huge tub, dumped in the bath salts provided and soaked for a long time in the perfumed water, trying not to think of tomorrow. Tomorrow when she'd be on her way back to wherever she came from. Instead of staying in a hotel in a room adjoining Parker's, anticipating an evening in his company, she'd be somewhere else, some*one* else. Just one more evening, she promised herself. Tomorrow she'd say goodbye to him and go back to her old life. Whatever it was.

But when Parker knocked on her door that evening, she suddenly knew it would be more of a problem than she'd thought. He was wearing a dark suit that fit as if it were made for him. His crisp white shirt contrasted with his dark hair. If she didn't know he was a sheep rancher she might have taken him for a stockbroker.

She didn't know how long she'd been standing in the doorway staring at him, she only knew he was staring back, his gaze traveling up and down her little black dress appreciatively. Finally she turned to close the drapes and he gasped.

"Wait a minute," he said, alarmed. "There's no back on that dress."

"I know," she said, returning to the door. She kept her voice matter-of-fact, but inside she was trembling. The last night, she thought. This is the last night to be a part of his life. Not a big part, but better than nothing. And tomorrow she would be nothing. Not to him anyway.

He reached around her to run his calloused palm along her back. "Won't you be cold?"

Cold? She'd never been warmer. That was a shiver of pleasure she felt. The heat from his hand blazed a trail up and down her spine. "I'm fine," she said breathlessly.

"You look fine," he said, his voice low and even. Fine, he thought. Was that all he could say? He had no words for how she looked. He was stunned into speechlessness. The dressed hugged her body, molded to the shape of her breasts, accentuated her waist and the curve of her hips. The sight of her bare back had startled him. Seduced him. Her skin was the color of cream and felt like satin to his touch. He didn't want to let go. He realized she wasn't wearing a bra. She couldn't be. He inhaled the scent from her skin—lilacs or lilies of the valley. He didn't know which was which. He only knew he couldn't get enough of it, or of her.

The sheepherders, his speech, heredity and environment were all forgotten. All he wanted to do was put both hands on her hips and ease her back into her room. Peel that dress off her and take her to bed. He wanted her with a fierce longing that scared the hell out of him. He had no idea what *she* wanted. No idea why she was coming to this dinner at all, let alone in a dress that would make him forget the words to his speech.

He hadn't wanted her to come tonight. He was afraid she'd be out of place at the dinner. He was afraid she'd get in the way of what he'd come to do. She made him forget what that was. He thought she liked him. Thought she found him attractive in some way. But he'd been wrong before. And he didn't want to be wrong again. It hurt too much.

He dropped his hands to his sides. "Ready?" he asked, his voice back to normal, almost.

She gave him a funny little half smile he took to mean yes and they took the elevator to the top floor of the hotel with the view of the city below and the sun setting behind the mountains in the distance. The room was full of old friends, strangers, wives and assorted sheep traders from out of state. Loud voices rose and filled the air. Laughter boomed and echoed off the walls.

He was quickly surrounded by men he hadn't seen in a long time. Some he'd forgotten, some he remembered. All of them were potential customers for his rams. They were pumping his hand, pounding his back and separating him from Christine.

Out of the corner of his eyes he saw Ted Lemke from Evergreen, his Stetson hat tilted to one side, offer to get Christine something to drink. He strained to hear what she said but couldn't. Ted left for the bar. Two men he didn't know approached her, engaged her in conversation. She was taken care of. Now it was his chance to do what he'd come to do. Wheel and deal sheep. He didn't have to worry about her. Didn't have to watch her from across the room. But he did. He managed to buy a breeding ram and sell two ewes and still keep her in view.

Somebody tapped a spoon against a drinking glass and the men and women in the room drifted toward the round tables. Parker dove through the crowd, took Christine firmly by the elbow and herded her like a stray lamb to the head table, aware that he'd interrupted a conversation between her and four ranchers he'd never seen before who were eyeing her as if she were up for sale herself.

"Everyone's so nice," she said, slanting a glance at him.

"Yeah. Real nice." He gripped her elbow a little tighter. They sat down. They ate shrimp cocktail, they ate chicken in some kind of sauce and wild rice. He didn't taste any of it. He was aware that her arm brushed his, that her back was bare, that her hair curled enticingly around her face. While he talked projected gains with the man on his right, he listened to her talk to the man on her left. He couldn't concentrate on the efficiency of rambouillets versus merinos with her there. He couldn't think of anything but her.

He should never have brought her along. He should have left her at the bus station in Clear Creek like the last time. He felt like a fool for worrying about her when it was obvious she could take care of herself now. When the dinner was finally over, the dishes had been cleared and the coffee cups refilled, he was introduced, and stood to give his speech.

He pulled some notes from his pocket and proceeded to talk. All the while he felt her eyes on him, knew she was watching him with wide gray eyes, lips parted slightly as if everything he said was fascinating and enthralling. Maybe it was. Maybe he was better than he thought he was.

There were questions afterward and then more time to mill around and talk. But he was tired of milling, tired of talking, tired of buying and selling. He found Christine and with his hand on her bare back he guided her out of the banquet room and into the crowded hall. Suddenly he was impatient. Impatient to get away from everybody. Impatient to get her alone. Too impatient to wait for the elevator.

"Want to walk down?" he asked.

She nodded then looked at her high-heeled shoes. "I'll take these off."

He bent over to help her. He slid his hand under her foot and took one shoe off. The blood rushed to his head. She stood on one stockinged foot and he removed the other shoe. His hand lingered, caressing the smooth instep, then the ball of her foot. He wanted more, so much more. But he stood and staggered backward.

"You okay?" she asked, reaching out to steady him.

"Sure," he said. But he leaned forward, until her lips were only inches from his. As if they were alone instead of surrounded by conventioneers.

"Thanks," she murmured. "I'm not used to..."

He straightened and gave her an amused look. "Men with foot fetishes?"

"Wearing high heels," she corrected.

With her shoes in one hand he opened the door to the stairwell and hand in hand they rushed down eight flights of stairs, arriving breathless at the fourth floor. At their respective doors, they hesitated.

"Want to come in?" she asked at last.

Her room was a mirror image of his. His gaze went to the large bed and stayed there. Images swam in front of his eyes. She was so lovely. So tempting. So sexy in that damned dress And so damned temporary. Because after tonight he would never see Christine again. He could not afford to lose his heart to her, because if he did, he'd never get it back again.

"Your speech was wonderful," she said, walking lightly to the window to open the curtains and gaze at the city lights that sparkled in the clear air. "I had no idea how much you knew about genetics."

"Uh-huh."

"All those studies you've done on twin sheep sound like the same kind that are done on humans."

"Christine."

Hearing the urgency in his voice, she turned to face him, her eyes brimming with questions.

"I don't want to talk about sheep." He crossed the room in two strides and she was in his arms where she belonged. She knew it. He knew it. With a frantic, fevered energy she matched him kiss for kiss, each one hungrier than the last. Her fingers sifted through his hair, and pulled him closer. She wanted more, as much as he could give. Deeper kisses, hotter kisses until her knees buckled. There was a loud roaring like thunder in his ears. Next they'd be on the floor. He preferred the bed. He picked her up and carried her there, his gaze never leaving hers.

When he laid her on the mauve bedspread, her black dress outlined the curves of her breasts, caressed her hips. He loosened his collar and caught her hands in his. "What do you want?" he asked, his heart banging against his ribs.

She pressed her hand against his chest and caught her breath. "You."

"What about tomorrow?"

"There is no tomorrow," she said simply. But suddenly her eyes clouded and shimmered with tears. "Tomorrow I'll be someone else." She shifted, propped herself on one elbow, causing a gap to form between the dress and the swell of her breasts. Then she ran her finger across his lips. Her touch set him on fire. He didn't care who she was, as long as she was his tonight. He kissed her fingers.

"Tonight you're mine," he said roughly.

The telephone rang. Parker froze. Christine stared up at him. Finally she groped for the receiver.

"Sarah," she said. "Is something wrong? How did you find me?" She pulled herself up against the headboard and Parker's face creased into a worried frown. "You did?" Christine held her hand over the mouthpiece. "She's fine," she whispered, and Parker breathed a sigh of relief.

"Yes, he's planning to see you, I think tomorrow." She looked up inquiringly and Parker nodded.

"At noon," he mouthed.

"Tomorrow at noon," she repeated. "How's that?" She paused.

"No, Sarah," Christine said. "I can't come. I've got... things I have to do. You remember I told you I have to find out about my past." She listened to Sarah talk about school for a few more minutes then she finally hung up.

Parker stood at the side of the bed. "How did she find you?" he asked.

"Rang your room and then when no one answered, the operator rang mine." Christine straightened the straps on her dress. "I'm not sure why she called. Just to check with you, I guess." She looked at Parker and felt him slipping away from her, physically and emotionally. If the phone hadn't rung, what would have happened? Would she have made love to Parker?

She wanted to desperately. Since the first time she'd seen him, felt his hands on her bruised body. Felt safe in his arms. But how could she make love with Parker, not knowing who she was or who MTT was? What if she was involved with someone else? What if she wasn't? Then she could have had one more night as a woman whose life had started in the middle of a sheep pasture, who only knew one thing for sure—she'd fallen in love with a rancher. At least she would have had one night to remember. This way she had nothing.

Nothing? What about cool mornings in the meadow with the dew still on the grass? The smell of coffee in the kitchen. The sound of laughter coming from the bunkhouse. The sight of Parker on his horse. The touch of his lips, his hands on her bare back. Yes, she had something to remember. Things she'd never forget.

He was pacing back and forth in front of the window. "Want me to come with you in the morning, wherever you're going?" he asked.

"Oh, no. I've already disrupted your life enough. I have the address of the Department of Missing Persons. So," she said brightly, "it looks like you're finally rid of me."

He stopped pacing and looked at her with narrowed eyes. "That sounds like goodbye."

She pressed her hand against her heart as if she could stop it from aching. "I suppose it is."

"Is that the way you want it?" he asked, his voice hardened into steel.

"It's not what I want, it's the way it is," she explained calmly. Then suddenly she blurted, all her frustration coming to the surface, "We have no future, you and I. Whatever there is between us would last one night. It would have been a one-night stand. Maybe you thought that's what I wanted." Maybe because that was what she wanted. "But what would happen after that? You'd go back to a life you love. But what have I got waiting for me?" Her voice broke. "I don't know."

He took a step backward, his jaw tightened. She knew he couldn't deny it. After tonight he'd return to his ranch and his family. He wouldn't give her a second thought. But she'd be hooked forever on Parker Robinson. No matter what she found out tomorrow, she knew he was the only man in her life. And he didn't want her in his life.

"When you find out," he said at last, "let me know."

"I'll do that," she said stiffly.

"Good night," he said, moving through the connecting door and closing it firmly behind him. Actually it was a cross between slamming and closing firmly.

The next morning Parker insisted on giving her a ride to the department. Numbly, she accepted. On their way through the lobby they passed a well-dressed woman on her way in. She stopped short and shrieked.

"Christine Austin! I can't believe my eyes."

Christine stopped and stared. The woman, a total stranger to her, threw her arms around Christine and kissed the air somewhere around Christine's ear. "What on earth are you doing here?" she demanded.

Before Christine could think up some kind of reasonable answer, the woman looked her up and down, taking in her Western-style checked shirt, jeans and shoes. "Don't tell me you're with the sheepherders?" She laughed merrily at the very idea. "The place is crawling with them, you know."

"I know," Christine murmured.

"So how was the camping trip? I take it you found the place all right?"

"Yes, yes," Christine said with a sideways glance at Parker.

The woman followed Christine's gaze and gave Parker a curious look. There was a brief awkward silence during which Christine should have introduced them, but couldn't. Then the woman continued.

"You look great," she told Christine. "You needed to get away from everything. After what you went through..."

Christine fought off the urge to ask what *had* she been through and simply nodded. "It's good seeing you again," she murmured, then edged her way toward the double doors with Parker at her side.

"Keep in touch," the woman called. "I'll tell everyone you're back."

Outside the glass double doors of the hotel, Christine stopped cold and faced Parker. "The past is catching up with me," she said, biting her lower lip.

He nodded, looking at her as if he'd never seen her before. She wrapped her arms around her waist, filled with an unbearable sadness. Unwilling to go forward, and unable to go backward, she just stood there, her gaze locked with Parker's. It was the end, and it was the beginning. Whatever happened, nothing would ever be the same. And they both knew it.

Chapter Eight

Parker drove slowly down a winding street with large houses set on wide, well-landscaped lots. He was looking for number 732 Canyon Street, the address listed in the phone book for Christine Austin. After the woman left and they'd finally recovered their senses that morning and returned to the hotel lobby, he and Christine went through the listings for Austin in Denver and found her there.

He glanced at her, but she had her face pressed to the window looking for what he presumed was her house. "There...there it is," she stammered, pointing to a three-story stone house at the end of the street.

He pulled up in front of the house and before he could get out, she'd jerked the car door open and was standing on the curb.

"Thanks for everything," she said, meeting his gaze only briefly before she turned and strode up the walk.

"Wait a minute," he called through the open window. But she didn't even turn around. She'd heard him, but she didn't look back. Was that the way it ended, with uncertainty and doubt, with nothing resolved? He sat in his car until she'd found a key under the mat, unlocked the door and disappeared into the house. Then he slowly drove away. Who was in there waiting for her? Who was there to take care of her, buy her clothes, eat the food she cooked? He would never know.

Like a ball of yarn unraveling, Christine's memory was coming back to her now, faster and faster, pell-mell, whether she liked it or not. As she walked up the cement path, staring at the pale gray stone house, she wondered if someone might wave from a window or come bursting out the front door to greet her. But no one did.

She stood on the front porch for a long moment, then reached without thinking for the key under the mat and unlocked the door. She knew Parker was still there, waiting and watching from the street. But she also knew he was not a part of her life anymore, any more than she was part of his.

She stepped over a pile of unopened mail into a cool, tiled foyer. Ignoring the mountain of correspondence, she continued to the living room with its stone fireplace and upholstered wing-backed chairs. In one corner there was a large library table stacked with presents of various shapes and sizes wrapped in silver and white. Wedding presents. Her wedding presents. But she wasn't married. She glanced at a card tucked under a white ribbon. "Christine and Michael."

Michael. There was no face to go with the name. Only feelings. Anger, shame and humiliation crowded together in her mind. She turned her back on the beautiful boxes and walked like a sleepwalker to the dining room, barely noticing the long cherrywood table with a vase of wilted flowers in the center. The kitchen was filled with gourmet cookware and shelves of cookbooks. The smell of cinnamon and spice hung faintly in the air. The windows looked out on a well-tended garden. Roses climbed the back fence. All strange and yet strangely familiar.

She took a jar of herbs from a shelf and inhaled the pungent smell. Scenes of dinner parties, memories of mixing, blending and baking in this room all came flooding back. Happy memories. She continued her wandering, up the stairs to her bedroom. Soft peach and pale green on the walls and on the bed a soft, flowered comforter. A desk with stationery, a stack of unfinished thank-you notes. A bookcase filled with volumes of poetry, short stories and literary classics.

She sat on the edge of the bed and stared out the window at the purple clematis climbing a trellis in the garden. Who was Christine Austin and what did she do besides cook and write notes and read? Why hadn't she gotten married? She didn't want to know, but she had to know. She walked to her desk and touched the playback button on the answering machine. So many messages, so many voices. And from them she pieced together a person—her; a life—hers.

Her mother was sorry, her friends were sorry. Sorry to hear the wedding was called off. They didn't say who'd called it off, but Christine knew. And suddenly she knew why. She didn't blame Michael. Who would want to marry a woman who couldn't have children? The scene in the doctor's office came rushing back to her as if it was yesterday instead of a week before the wedding. The smell of antiseptic. X rays. Test results. The words "unrepairable fallopian tube damage" and the humiliation. No wonder she'd clung to her amnesia, unwilling to face the past. She almost wished she'd never recovered her memory. As if not knowing would make it not so.

She'd never forget the look on Michael's face when she told him. The shock and the sorrow. Of course there were other possibilities. Other ways to make a baby. Donors or surrogates, but all were fraught with problems. And Michael had enough problems to deal with already. His family. His business. This was the last straw. She didn't blame him. Even now, standing at her desk, looking at a picture of his handsome face, she knew he'd had no choice.

Michael Taylor Thomas IV was expected to produce Michael Taylor Thomas V. Who would be expected to step into his father's shoes at the firm as Michael had. But she had choices. Adoption was one of them. Someday. She would find a way. Because she wanted kids. More than anything. She'd always wanted them. Michael knew that and yet when she told him he could only think of himself and his obligation. Not to her, but to his family. It was only natural with a family like his, she told herself. He would find someone else, someone whose fertility was intact. And she...she would do what she had to do.

She picked up the telephone. Made a few calls. Only to people who sounded genuinely worried. Her mother, a few friends, the hospital where she volunteered. Told them all she'd been vacationing at a ranch.

"One of those places where you dress up like a cowboy and drive the cattle to Montana?" her mother inquired.

"No, Mother. It was a sheep ranch in the middle of a valley. But I did help out some, cooking, gardening, riding."

"How did you find it?" her mother asked.

Christine rubbed her head. "I left my car, oh . . . my car. Yes, anyway I left it at the entrance to this campground and I hiked in with my tent and backpack and stumbled onto private property, only I didn't know it." The memories were flooding back as she talked.

"You must give me the name of the ranch," her mother said. "Someone at the Garden Club the other day was looking for a place like that to stay, where they take guests and she can feel at one with the soil and nature."

Christine smiled. "I will. When I unpack and get back to normal." Whatever that was. Was it normal to do nothing but volunteer work, social engagements and wedding preparations? If so, what happened when the wedding was called off and the round of parties that filled her calendar were no longer appealing?

"Are you . . . have you spoken to Michael?" her mother asked hesitantly.

"Not yet. I just got back. I'm just sorry it had to end like that."

"Maybe it isn't over," her mother suggested hopefully.

"It *is* over," Christine said firmly.

"I was afraid you'd say that. Well, we'll talk about it at lunch. Thursday?" she asked.

"Fine."

For the next few days she wandered restlessly through the house, picturing Parker at the hotel, surrounded by old friends, too busy to think of her. She must get busy, too, so she wouldn't think of him. But busy doing what? She had no job. She lived off a trust fund established by her grandfather.

She wrote a check to Parker and sent it to the ranch to cover all the money he'd lent her. She enclosed a brief note saying her memory was coming back. That she'd found friends and family and thanked him very much for his help. She didn't tell him she'd been left at the altar, didn't mention her infertility or her frivolous lifestyle.

Compared to raising sheep, her activities seemed useless and shallow. She was glad he couldn't see her attending board meetings or lunching with friends. The one thing she was proud of was her volunteer work in the pediatrics wing of the local hospital. She wouldn't mind if he saw her in her pink smock reading stories to preschoolers, rocking AIDS babies or feeding preemies.

That Thursday, after having lunch with her mother, she returned home to find a message from Sarah on her machine. Immediately she called her back.

"Sarah," she said, "how did you find me?"

"My dad told me your last name so I looked it up in the phone book. Where do you live anyway?"

Christine smiled at the sound of the girl's voice. "I live on Canyon Road right here in Denver. I have a house and a car and even a mother...and I've got my memory back."

"That is so-oo cool. I can't wait to hear all about it. Come and see me this weekend."

How like her to command instead of ask, Christine thought. "You're not going home for the weekend?"

"No, cuz it's our spring festival. I have to be here. I'm in the chorus and we're singing. Come Friday after school. I get out at three-thirty."

"Okay. I'm looking forward to seeing you."

"I thought you'd forgotten me," Sarah said, suddenly sober.

"Of course I didn't. But it took me a while to... to get readjusted." As if she'd ever be readjusted to this strange life.

"My dad thought so, too."

"He thought I'd forgotten you?"

"He thinks you've forgotten *him*."

"But I sent him some money and wrote him a note."

"He read it to me. It didn't say very much."

Christine looked out her bedroom window across the treetops. What did he expect? That she'd pour out her heart, tell him how much she missed him, how much she loved him? She wasn't that far gone. She still had a little pride.

"You're not married, are you?" Sarah asked.

"No, I'm not."

"Good. See ya." And she hung up.

Before Sarah's spring festival Christine went back to her old hairdresser who shook her head in despair when she ran her comb through Christine's hair.

With her hair turned into a halo of professionally trimmed curls and wearing a pearl gray hand-knit sweater that matched her mid-calf-length skirt Christine drove to the school. Behind the gates were spacious lawns and attractive brick buildings. At the office she asked for Sarah.

"Are you here for parents' day?" the woman asked Christine after she'd placed a brief phone call to Sarah's dorm.

Christine paused. "No, I'm here to see a friend." Before she could wonder why Sarah hadn't told her it was parents' day, the girl came flying across the campus and threw herself into Christine's arms.

"I'm so glad to see you," Sarah said breathlessly. "Christine Austin," she said, her bright eyes looking her up and down. "You've got a last name now and some nice new clothes. Did you ever find out how old you are?"

"I'm thirty-one. Doesn't that seem old?"

"Uh-uh. It's just right." Sarah grabbed her hand and led her on a tour of the campus.

"This is a beautiful place," Christine noted as they walked past a grove of aspen trees toward the sports complex.

Sarah wrinkled her nose. "You think so?" she asked. "I'd rather be home."

"Well, summer vacation isn't far off, is it?"

"Three weeks. But I'm not coming back in the fall," Sarah said with the determined tone Christine remembered so well.

"Does your father know that?" Christine asked, pausing to look into Sarah's blue eyes.

"I've told him, but he doesn't believe me." She tilted her head. "I was hoping you'd talk to him."

"Talk to him? I don't think I'll have a chance to talk to him."

"Yes, you will. At dinner tonight. He's coming for parents' weekend. You're allowed two guests. For your mom and dad." She shrugged. "You're not my mom, but..."

"Wait a minute," Christine said, her heart hammering at the idea of seeing Parker. "If you brought me here to talk your dad into letting you move home, it's not going to work. What makes you think he'll listen to me?"

"Cuz he likes you."

"Sarah."

"And he misses you."

Christine took Sarah by the shoulders. "He doesn't miss me. I was only there a few weeks. You wish he missed me, maybe I wish he did, too, but he doesn't."

"Okay," Sarah agreed, to humor her. "But tonight you'll see. I'm going to ask him. Come on." She tugged at Christine's hand. "You have to see my dorm. My roommate wants to meet you. She's got a stepmother, too."

After she'd toured the dorms and met Sarah's friends, and shadows crossed the wide, well-kept lawns, Christine formed an excuse in her mind, and prepared to leave before it was too late. But it *was* too late. Parker was already briskly striding around the corner of the administration building as they were coming toward him. Before she ran into him, Christine stopped abruptly. Parker stopped dead in his tracks and stared at Christine as if he'd seen a ghost. He was dressed in city clothes, tailored slacks, a striped tie and a jacket. From the shocked look on his face, he didn't know she'd be there.

Christine was vaguely aware of Sarah watching the two of them and grinning impishly. She tried to speak but the words caught in her throat. And her heart missed every other beat. Why had she come? Why hadn't she foreseen this?

"I didn't expect to see you," he said at last. He didn't say "ever again," but she knew that's what he meant. His voice was a shade deeper than she remembered, his shoulders a little broader, his eyes even bluer. Did he have to be so damnably good-looking? "You've changed," he said, his eyes taking a tour from her shiny curls to her expensive suede shoes. He didn't say "for the worse," but she wondered if that's what he meant. What did he expect? That she'd show up in jeans and a checked shirt?

"It's been a while," she said brightly.

Ten days, he thought, but who's counting? He clenched his fists together to keep from taking her in his arms. Right there in front of Sarah. Ten days since she'd said goodbye. Ten days telling himself he'd better get used to being without her because he was never going to see her again. And now she was here, but she wasn't the same woman he'd known at the ranch. This woman had clearly found herself. What *did* she find? Who was she? All he knew was her last name and that she had friends and family. What did that mean?

As if she'd read his mind, his daughter piped up, "She's not married, Dad."

They both looked at her and after a brief, awkward pause, they laughed. It broke the tension. And encouraged Sarah to elaborate. "And she's thirty-one years old. Just what I thought when I looked at her teeth," she said smugly.

Parker looked at Christine. Unmarried at thirty-one. While they walked together toward the cafeteria he wondered why someone hadn't snatched her up by now. Inside the brightly lighted room they found chairs at one of the long tables set up for dinner. They sat on either side of Sarah who couldn't stop smiling and waving to her friends. He glanced at Christine's left hand. No ring. Sarah said she wasn't married, but he just wanted to check. Not that it mattered to him. She probably had a good reason for staying single, just as he did.

What was important was that she was back where she belonged. He had a few questions to ask her, but with

Sarah between them, listening to every word they said, he couldn't risk coming off looking too interested. Still, as the dinner wore on and was followed by speeches from the headmistress and the dean, his curiosity consumed him.

He draped his arm across Sarah's chair and his fingers brushed Christine's sleeve. He leaned back in his chair. She leaned back in hers and slanted a glance in his direction. "How are you?" he asked. How inane. After sitting there for two hours, was that all he could come up with?

She smiled brightly. "Fine."

Sarah went to join the girls' chorus and Parker tried again. It should be easier without Sarah between them. "What happened . . . after I left?"

"I went up to the house, *my* house and I let myself in. It was so weird, trying to imagine living there."

"And your memory?"

"It came back, just as the doctor said it would, in bits and pieces. There are still things I don't remember, like faces, names and phone numbers."

"What about the recent past, do you still remember the ranch?" he asked, as if the return of her long-term memory might have erased what had just happened. He had to know for sure.

"Your ranch? Of course I do. I remember the swing on the front porch, the smell of wet grass, the cold water in the brook." Her gray eyes grew soft and luminous as she reminisced. He let his fingers linger on her shoulder, let his gaze wander to the swell of her breasts under the soft sweater. Wishing he could take her home with him, back to the smell of wet grass, to the porch swing and crush her to him, slide his hands up under that soft sweater and finish what they'd started. He was breathing hard now. He should never have come to-night. If he'd known she'd be there... if he'd known she'd look like she did. So familiar and yet so different. As if she'd been polished, from her hair to her fingertips, like a shiny apple. A delicious, irresistible apple. One that was out of his grasp.

"It's lambswool," she said, following his gaze.

"What? Yes, I know. Who do you live with?" he asked, jerking his gaze back to hers.

"No one," she said. Was there a trace of sadness in her voice or did he just imagine it?

"That's good," he said with relief. "You don't have to share the kitchen. You've got your own bed... bedroom." All he could think about was the bed in the hotel where they'd almost made love and he wondered if the color that suddenly tinted her cheeks meant she remembered, too.

"What do you do?" he asked.

She looked down and smoothed a crease in her skirt. "The only really worthwhile thing I do is work in the pediatrics ward of the hospital. I really love the kids and I guess they like me, too."

"You mean, you're a nurse."

"No, I'm not anything." She gave him a small embarrassed smile.

"Not a teacher, not a poet or a professional cook?"

"No, just a dilettante. A dabbler. I cook, I read poetry and I ride a horse I board at a stable. But not professionally. I live on a small trust fund so I don't really need to work." Again, the embarrassed little smile.

"Nothing wrong with that," he said.

"What about you?" she said, pressing her fingers together. "Did you have any luck at the meeting?"

"Yeah. As a matter of fact I picked up some good breeding stock. The bad news is, while I was gone the cook quit."

Her mouth turned down at the corners. "Oh, no."

"Oh, well." He picked up his dessert fork and tapped it absently on the table. "It's always something."

"Yes, it is, isn't it," she agreed, then turned her chair so she could see Sarah as the chorus filed onto the stage.

Parker studied her profile, her straight nose, high cheekbones and firm chin, admired the way her hair framed her face in little tendrils. He knew how soft it felt, how silky. Was that why he couldn't forget her? Her hair, her face? No, it was more than that. It was the way she bit her lip when she was concentrating. The way she wrinkled her nose when she was worried. It was the way she turned his house into a home again. The smell of her soap, the smell of her cooking. It was all these things and more.

That didn't mean he couldn't forget her. He had to. She had her own life now, one that had nothing to do with his ranch. When the singers took a break, he pulled his chair closer to hers. "Pop asked about you."

"Tell him I miss him, and all those wonderful stories he tells."

"What'll I tell him when he asks if you're ever coming back?"

"Parker..." There was a pained look in her eyes. "Haven't we been through this before?"

"Never mind. I can see you've got your life back and that's good."

"I guess so." She twisted her napkin in her lap. "Sometimes I wonder what it's all about."

"Your life?" he asked, raising his eyebrows. "Don't you know?"

"Not yet. Maybe it will come to me. But when I wake up in the morning sometimes I don't know what I'm supposed to do." She glanced up at him, and when she saw the unwanted sympathy in his eyes she quickly continued. "Then I look at my calendar and I know." Her lips curved upward, but her eyes were still sad and troubled.

"What about the diamond pendant?" he asked. "Did you find out who MTT was?"

She stared at the empty stage as if willing the music to start so she wouldn't have to answer. "Yes," she said finally.

"Well?"

She sighed. "The man I was engaged to."

"Was?"

"It's over."

He tried to conceal the relief that flooded his chest. Was this broken engagement the reason for the sadness in her eyes?

Christine turned her head in his direction and changed the subject. "Sarah's looking forward to coming home for the summer. I guess you know she doesn't want to come back here in the fall. I can understand how she feels. I was sent away to school, too."

"I take it you didn't like it."

She shook her head. "I probably made my parents' lives miserable, too, just the way Sarah's doing. Anyway, she asked me to ask you, and now I've done it. I knew what you'd say."

"Am I that predictable?" he asked, leaning forward as someone came around to refill the coffee cups.

Christine gave him a quick glance and the memories came flooding back. Of all the times he'd surprised her, caught her off guard. Catching her as she slid off her horse at the pond, tying her apron in the kitchen, taking her shoes off after the hotel banquet. No, he wasn't all that predictable. But this wasn't the time to tell him. That time was never. Because if she told him that, he might think she couldn't forget him, that it meant too much to her, that she'd fallen in love with him. It was better for him to think she had a happy new life, when the truth was she was as homesick for the ranch as she'd ever been at boarding school. Ached with homesickness for the swing on the front porch, the newborn lambs frolicking on the lawn and, most of all, for Parker.

He was still looking at her, waiting for an answer to his question. "Predictable?" she repeated. "In some ways. In others..." She dragged her eyes from his, afraid he'd see the longing, the desire, she couldn't conceal.

Fortunately the music started up just then and she watched Sarah standing tall in the back row. She sang alto, and as she sang she watched her father and Christine with a small anxious expression in her blue eyes that Christine could see all the way across the room. Was it just changing schools that concerned her, going home or was it something else? Some other dream she was afraid wasn't going to come true.

When the program was over, and the audience clapped appreciatively, Sarah rushed back to the table where Christine and her father were standing waiting for her. She linked arms with both of them and they walked her back to her dorm.

To her credit, Sarah didn't ask or beg her father to let her come home. But when she said goodbye to them, she winked at Christine as if they were fellow conspirators. Christine wanted to tell her he'd said no and that he'd always say no, but she didn't have the heart to spoil the moment. She'd call her on the telephone and tell her next week.

"Thanks for coming," she said, hugging Christine. "Will you call me sometime?"

Christine promised, then she found herself walking through the school grounds in the dark toward the parking lot with Parker at her side. He didn't say anything. Neither did she. She thought they'd probably said everything they had to say.

But the silence went on too long, weighed too heavily on her, until Christine finally blurted, "She's a wonderful girl. You're very lucky, you know." What she wouldn't give for a daughter or a son.

"She likes you, too," he said, walking her to her car.

"I hope you don't mind my intruding on your parent weekend. When Sarah invited me, I didn't know."

"Of course not. It was good to see you again."

He sounded so formal, so polite, she wanted to scream. Good? Was that all it was, good to see her? While she broke out in a sweat, her heart did a double flip, her palms stuck to her skirt, for him it was just "good to see you again." Damn him for being so much in control.

He took the car keys out of her hand and unlocked her door for her. "Could we go somewhere and talk?" he asked, leaning against her car door.

"Haven't we been somewhere talking?" she asked. "And don't you have a long drive home?"

"I'm not going back tonight. I have a meeting tomorrow with Sarah's teachers. A progress report. I'm staying at a hotel."

"The same hotel where we..."

"No, a different one."

Christine looked up at his face, half-shadowed in the yellow glow from the sodium-vapor parking lot light. His eyes were pools of dark blue, so deep she felt she could drown in them. She had no clue as to why he wanted to talk more. But she knew she couldn't get in her car and say good-night, because she knew it would be goodbye. This time for good. And besides, she owed him a debt of hospitality. A debt a cup of coffee wouldn't quite repay. But it was a start. "Would you like to stop by my house? I could make a cup of coffee," she offered, suddenly feeling shy.

He hesitated only a second. "Sure?"

"Yes, of course. Why don't you follow me."

As she drove down the side streets with his headlights reflected in her rearview mirror, she wished she'd suggested a coffeehouse, or a pub. Oh, no, she had to invite him to her house for coffee in a halfhearted attempt to repay him for saving her life. When he suggested going someplace to talk she should have pleaded a sudden headache or maybe a touch of a contagious virus. What she really had was an attack of the jitters, that got worse the closer they got to her house. Her hands were clammy on the steering wheel just thinking of him assessing the house she lived in. When she pulled into her driveway, he pulled in behind her and she was trapped. It was too late for a headache, much too late for smallpox. And as soon as he walked in the front door he'd see how very different they really were. As if he didn't know it already.

Chapter Nine

Parker glanced up at the imposing three-story house. *Well, what did you expect?* he asked himself. *That she'd live in a shack?* Not a shack, he thought as she opened the front door and he followed her into the living room, but not a sophisticated town house either.

"Nice place you've got here," he said.

She looked around as if seeing it for the first time. "I suppose so. It's funny. Sometimes I feel like an impostor, like I don't really belong here." She twisted her fingers together. "But of course I do." She looked at the thermostat on the wall and turned the heat up a notch. "What they say about lightning victims is that life is never the same afterward. Maybe that's what's wrong with me."

"You don't look like anything's wrong with you," he assured her. She looked lovely, sophisticated, completely at home, the soft gray of her sweater blending with the pale shades of the wainscoting.

She led the way into the kitchen. There was nothing warm and cozy about it, but from what he could see she had every convenience imaginable, including the espresso machine she'd turned on. "Is this where you got all your cooking expertise?" he asked.

"I took a course at the culinary academy," she explained. "But I didn't graduate. I was never a professional. Anything."

"Is that important to you?" he asked.

"I'd like to feel useful," she said.

"And you don't?"

She shrugged. "Cappuccino? Latté?" she asked, measuring coffee from a package in the freezer.

"Fine," he said absently.

He straddled one of her straight-backed kitchen chairs, probably an original Shaker design, and watched her make coffee. Just the way he used to watch her work in his old, large, well-worn ranch kitchen, and yet everything had changed. She brought the steaming cups to the table, sat down across from him and looked up questioningly. Waiting to hear what he wanted to talk about.

"You know, I was almost going to ask you to come back and cook for me again." He laughed, but it sounded hollow in his ears. "Pretty ridiculous, huh?"

"Why?"

"Why, because a woman like you belongs in a place like this. Not on an isolated sheep ranch with nothing to do."

"Parker, how do you know where I belong? I don't even know myself. All I know is that I was happier on your ranch than I've ever been in my life. And I had plenty to do."

"For how long?" he demanded. "You were there a couple of weeks. My ex-wife lasted a year."

"I remind you of her, don't I? That's why you're afraid—"

He shoved his chair back and got to his feet. "I'm not afraid of anything. Especially not afraid to learn from my mistakes. I've made plenty of them. And I'll make plenty more, but not the same ones. I'll never get married again, and never subject another woman to my lifestyle again."

She jumped up and faced him, her eyes blazing. "Who asked you to anyway? Not me. Go ahead and live your life the way you want. You don't have to justify it to me or anybody. You're completely self-sufficient, you've got everything you want, except a cook. But you won't ask me to cook for you because you might end up liking me, you might even end up loving me." Her voice rose. She stopped and stared at him, her face burning, looking like she wished she could snatch the words back out of the air where they hung between them.

There was a loud roaring in his ears like the sound of an avalanche. With a sudden lunge of emotion he shoved the table aside, knocking the cups over, spilling the coffee, and he grabbed her by the shoulders. This was no time for words. There'd been too many already. And this was no time to think, either. Her eyes widened. Her pupils dilated. He took her mouth with one hard, hungry kiss. He forced her lips open and plunged his tongue to stake his claim, stroking, exploring, savoring the taste of her. With his hands tangled in her silky curls, he held her prisoner to his passion. And he didn't care. She'd pushed him over the edge. From the beginning. And now this.

When she moaned in the back of her throat he ran his hands down her back, pressing her to him, wanting to possess her, to make her his, let her know what she did to him, forgetting everything he'd ever said, everything he believed. Only aware of one thing, the need, the steaming pent-up desire that swirled around them in that cool clean gourmet kitchen.

She didn't pull away. She could have but she didn't. She returned his kisses, one after another, each one deeper, harder, faster. Her hands were around his neck, sifting through his hair. This time *he* groaned. He wanted her, all of her. He lifted her sweater. Without breaking the kiss, he cupped her breasts, felt the heat, felt them strain to escape from the wisps of her silk and lace bra. He felt the buds tighten under his calloused fingers. He knew how they'd look, how they'd feel in his hands, how they'd taste. Her lips were moving against his.

"Yes," she whispered. "Yes, yes, yes..."

He lifted her off her feet, and carried her into the living room. He'd done this before. At his house. He'd carried her from the bath to the bed that night. The past blended with the present. This time he wouldn't leave. If he could find the bedroom. She was no help. She'd angled her face to meet his, to tempt him, to kiss the corners of his mouth, his eyes, his ears until his knees buckled and he had to stop at the off-white sofa in the living room. They fell on it together. She was on top of him, her sweater twisted to one side, his face pressed against her flat stomach. He couldn't breathe. Didn't care. He reached for her bra but she got there first, unsnapping it for him.

Christine had ceased to think. Since her outburst she'd lost control. So had Parker. That left nobody in control and that was fine with her. All she knew was how much she wanted him. It didn't matter how, it didn't matter where. But it had to be now. Before she burned up with the fire that consumed her and there was nothing left but a tiny heap of ashes. She thrust the sweater over her head. Then she went for the buttons on his shirt. But he was in the way, and she was getting desperate. When his mouth took the taut peak of one aching breast she dug her fingernails into her palms and shuddered with pleasure. She felt she just might explode into tiny pieces of light.

With clumsy fingers he slid her skirt over her hips. She helped with the slip and the stockings and her silk bikini. And still he was dressed. She wanted to see him, feel his skin, taste him as he tasted her. All of him. She was frantic. But he wouldn't let her go. His hands pressed down on hers, his eyes bored into hers, blazing fire, blazing passion and need. And something else, something she'd never seen before, anywhere, ever.

This was no time to wonder what it was. No time to ask where it was leading. Somewhere in the back of her mind she knew he'd be sorry for this, just as she knew she wouldn't. The flames were too hot, the pleasure too intense, the need too great to feel regret. Not now, not ever. He slid his hands under her hips and lifted her up to him. Giving him access to her most intimate secrets. Her skin burned as his kisses trailed across her stomach and continued on downward. She gripped the edge of the cushion beneath her, and arched her body, unable to wait, unable to breathe.

And then she remembered. With the clarity her mind had lacked before, she knew why she couldn't continue to encourage Parker. He wanted more children. He'd expected a boy when Sarah was born, Emilio wanted a grandson to carry on the name, inherit the land. She couldn't have children, but Parker didn't know that. She had to tell him. But she couldn't. Not now. She could only pull back and withdraw. It wasn't fair to lead him on and then tell him she was infertile. She covered her face with her hands and pulled herself to a sitting position.

Parker froze. Despite the efficient central heating, a chill fell over the room. He felt like he'd been kicked in the gut by a six-hundred ram. Something was wrong. Something had changed. While he was losing himself in the wonder of her body, she was pulling away from him, mentally and physically. And he didn't know why. He pressed his knee into the couch and stood. He didn't look at her. He couldn't.

"What's wrong?" he demanded, shoving his shirt into his pants.

She didn't answer. She sat up and gathered her clothes from the floor as if nothing had happened. "Nothing. I just don't think we ought to be making love at this point in our relationship."

"Our *relationship?* Is that what you call it?"

When he finally glanced at her, she'd pulled her sweater over her head and had her skirt in her lap. Her hair clung to her forehead in damp tendrils, her mouth was red and swollen from their kisses. He didn't know how she felt or what she wanted. All he knew was that she didn't want to make love with him. And it was a good bet she wanted him out of there. But he had something else to say first.

"You at least owe me an explanation, don't you think? Of what's going on here. Something that makes a little more sense. I'm accustomed to women walking out on me with no explanation, but I expect more from you. Or I did.''

"Wait a minute,'' she said, wadding her clothes into a ball in her hands. "You don't know me at all. Not anymore. You never will, either, because you're only interested in what happened to you. Not in me. Not in Sarah. You can't accept her for what she is because she's not what you want her to be. With me it doesn't matter. I'm not part of your life. We can walk away from each other right now and it won't matter to either of us. But it matters to Sarah. She's your daughter and she's more like you than you know. If you weren't so pigheaded stubborn, you'd see it.'' Her cheeks burned and her eyes blurred with anger.

Parker stared at her, struck dumb by her words. How she'd turned what happened here tonight to an indictment of his treatment of Sarah was more than he could fathom. Then he left. Walked out of her house and out of her life.

Christine buried her head in her hands. She'd heard his footsteps, heard the door close behind him and his car start up. Then the tears came. Flowed like water, soaking her skirt and sweater. What a way for it to end. With her past coming back into her life to ruin her future. As if she had a future with Parker. She didn't. Especially now, after she realized that no man wants a woman who can't bear his children. She should have told him, but it was too painful to talk about it. All he really needed to know was that they weren't right for each other. And he definitely must realize that by now. She'd been angry, but she meant every word she'd said, and she wasn't sorry she'd said them.

She took a shower and went to bed, but not to sleep. She'd broken off with Parker for good. She wouldn't apologize. She wouldn't have the chance. He was angry. Angry and puzzled. She didn't blame him. He wasn't expecting a tirade from her. Somehow a tirade had been easier than the sad truth. And yet she couldn't forget the look on his face before he left. Surprise, hurt and anger.

Parker didn't sleep, either. He paced his hotel room until dawn. He replayed every word she'd said, and nothing made any sense. She wanted him and he wanted her. He didn't know where they were going with their "relationship" but he wanted to find out. Evidently she didn't. He relived every hungry kiss and every touch until his brain had turned to mush and his body begged for mercy.

She was wrong about one thing. They could walk away from each other, but it did matter, at least to him. He'd missed her. He missed her now. And she wasn't right about how he felt about Sarah. He only wanted what was best for her. How could Christine know what that was? How could she understand how a parent felt if she had no children of her own? He finally took a hot shower and got dressed for his appointment with the headmistress.

His head felt twice the size of the soccer ball the girls' team was kicking on the green field in front of the office. He'd feel better when he had his conference. It always gave him a warm glow to hear how well his daughter was doing. It reinforced his decision to send her away to school. Enabled him to stick to his plan of keeping her there despite her protests.

He straightened his tie, glad he'd brought an extra since the one he'd worn last night looked like it had been balled up and mashed by the fashion police along with his shirt and pants. For a fleeting moment he wondered what condition Christine's soft gray sweater was in, and her silk and lace bra, then he took a deep breath and walked into the office. He stopped in his tracks. Instead of just the headmistress, the dean and the school counselor were waiting for him.

"Sit down, Mr. Robinson," the headmistress said without a trace of a smile. "I'm sorry this meeting can't be as positive as those we've had in the past."

He sat down feeling light-headed and confused.

"I'm afraid Sarah's broken one of our important rules," the counselor interjected, her eyes fastened on him.

"But I just saw her last night," he protested.

"Yes, we understand. At that time you told Sarah there was no chance she would not be continuing at the Academy next year, is that right?"

"Of course."

"When she returned to her dorm she evidently brought out a package of cigarettes and smoked one."

Parker stared at the woman in disbelief. "But she doesn't smoke," he said.

"Which explains why she was coughing so badly when the dorm was evacuated."

"Evacuated?" he said, still stunned.

"After the fire alarm went off," the headmistress explained.

"They're very sensitive," the counselor interjected.

"And the fire department arrived."

"Oh, my God."

"Our sentiments exactly. The school, being built in the last century, is composed of many historic buildings, as you are aware, which are extremely vulnerable to fire and other natural disasters. Unaccustomed to smoking as she is, your daughter might have left the cigarette burning ... and any number of catastrophes might have occurred, including loss of property or even life. Nothing happened except that the local fire department spent their valuable time and considerable efforts to come to our aid and all of us here endured a severe scare. It's what could have happened that really frightens us.''

"Of course,'' Parker said. His daughter. No matter how high-spirited, how mischievous, she'd never done anything like this before. "What ... what kind of punishment ...''

"There's only one thing to be done in a case like this,'' the headmistress said. "The rules are clear. Immediate expulsion.''

Parker gasped.

The counselor held one hand up. "But in view of her excellent academic record, we want her to complete her school year. Perhaps at home under your supervision? We will send all materials with Sarah, as well as her final examinations, with the understanding she'll be monitored.''

"Of course,'' Parker muttered, having no idea how he'd accomplish that. Maybe his father ...

"As disturbing as this must be to you and to all of us here at the Academy,'' the counselor said, "Sarah herself did not seem overly upset at the idea of returning home. Often in these cases of aberrant behavior, where a model student suddenly breaks out of the mold, we notice a desperate bid on the part of the child for attention.''

Parker nodded slowly. "I have to accept some blame in this. She hasn't been completely happy here, which is not at all the fault of your school,'' he assured the women. "It's more than homesickness, but... it's too complicated to explain. I thank you for your understanding." He shook hands before he left the room, feeling hollow and empty inside. Why, why, why? he asked himself. But he knew the answer.

Sarah was sitting on the front steps of her dorm, surrounded by boxes and suitcases, with her head on her knees. Parker's aching head was full of conflicting emotions: guilt, anger, shame and now sympathy. She looked so small and alone there in front of the imposing old frame building. But when she looked up there was defiance in her blue gaze and a trace of fear.

He held out his arms and she hesitated only a moment before she rushed into them. "I'm sorry," she sobbed against his chest. "I didn't mean to cause an uproar," she said.

"What did you mean to do?" he asked with his hand smoothing her hair, as if he didn't know.

"Get sent home."

"Well, you got your wish," he said dryly. Then he looked down into her tear-streaked face. "Do you know you could have burned the dorm down, including your classmates?"

"With one cigarette?" she asked, round-eyed.

"It's happened. One cigarette carelessly left near flammable materials. I know that's not what you had in mind. And thank God it didn't happen. But it was an irresponsible and dangerous thing to do. Smoking is clearly against the rules. You knew that. I guess that's why you did it."

"I hate it here," she declared. "I hate the rules, the dorm, the food. I hate the city and the way we're cooped up in there," she blurted, and then she started to cry in earnest. With one arm around her shoulders he led her to the car, settled her in the front seat with his large clean handkerchief, then he loaded her suitcases and boxes into the trunk. And as they drove away past green lawns and brick buildings he knew he would have hated it, too, if he'd had to go there. She'd said all those things to him before, but he hadn't listened to her. Not really. So she took desperate measures.

"I understand," he said. It was wrong of her, but he really did understand why she did it.

She leaned her head back and looked up at him, her cheeks stained with tears. "What are you going to do to me?"

"Take you home."

"What about school?"

"They said you'll get credit for this year if you do the work and pass the tests. As long as someone supervises you. As for next year, I don't know. I'm going back to the hotel and check out. I'll give Pop a call and tell him we're coming. Maybe he..."

"Sure, Pop can be my teacher," she said with a watery smile.

Parker nodded, but he couldn't expect the old man to keep up with Sarah, to discipline her, make her study, keep her in the house. He was putty in her hands, always had been... the perfect grandfather, kind and loving and spoiling her every minute he could. Her own pony, a pet lamb, baby chicks, a swing set... whatever she wanted.

He did call the ranch, though, to prepare his father for their arrival. Dusty answered the phone. "Your pop is in town at Doc Haller's having his leg set. Yep, he fell off the hitching post watching the men branding. Mac drove him in. It's not too bad, they said, ought to be up and around in his cast and crutches . . . oh, in a month or two. Till then, got to stay put." ˉ

Parker stood staring at the telephone in the hotel lobby wondering what else could go wrong today. He didn't have to wait much longer to find out.

"Oh, yeah, three of the men are gonna quit. Jack Spade, Lionel and Lucky. Got their bags packed. Less you come back with a cook. Told 'em that's not what you was doing in Denver, hiring a new cook, but they got it in their mind. Well, just thought you ought to know."

"Thanks." Parker stared out the window at the cars whizzing by, at the concrete city out there with the mountains in the distance. "Look," he said, "tell them I'll get a cook. If I have to kidnap one from the culinary academy." Then he hung up and looked around the lobby. Sarah was in the coffee shop having breakfast, eating with the ravenous appetite of a child who knows she's going home.

The words "culinary academy" reminded him of Christine. But then everything reminded him of her. Everything in the city, everything at the ranch. He remembered how she said she'd been happier at the ranch than anywhere in her life. When she was there she made everyone else happy, too, Sarah, the men, his father . . . and Parker, too. But would she come back if he asked her? Not likely, not after last night. If he begged her? If he apologized for whatever it was he'd done? If he promised not to come on to her?

All he could do was try. All he had to lose was his pride. His self-respect. He looked up her number in the phone book. His palm stuck to the receiver. The sweat beaded on his forehead as he punched in the numbers with his finger. When she finally answered she sounded as tired as he felt.

"Christine, it's Parker. I'm in a jam."

"What kind of jam?" she asked.

"Every kind you can think of. Sarah got kicked out of school." Christine gasped but he continued. "My dad broke his leg and the men are going to quit if I don't bring home a cook."

"Yes?"

Couldn't she say something besides yes? Couldn't she show some sympathy? Apparently not. "I need someone to supervise Sarah's homework so she can finish out the school year and I need someone to cook. I need you. And I need you now." She didn't say anything. He couldn't keep the desperation out of his voice. "It would just be until June. Look, I know you weren't happy with the way our relationship—" he almost choked on the word "—was going. You made that perfectly clear. And I know you've probably got other people in your life, other options, but nobody needs you as much as I do. They couldn't. And it will be strictly business, I promise."

"Where are you?" she asked. "Where's Sarah? Is she all right?"

"We're at the hotel. Sarah's a little subdued considering what happened, but she's all right."

"What happened? Never mind. I'll come."

"You'll come?" Relief flooded his body. "Are you sure? I'll pick you up."

"I'll take my own car. I'll leave this afternoon."

Her own car. That way she could leave whenever she wanted to. It made sense. And yet it hurt. It was déjà vu all over again. "Thanks, Christine."

"You're welcome."

She sounded cool, detached, and yet she was coming. It was more than he'd hoped for, more than he'd expected and definitely more than he deserved. His father was in a cast, his daughter was expelled and his men were about to quit, but he smiled all the way to the coffee shop where he joined Sarah for a very large breakfast, and told her the news.

Christine tossed her jeans and cotton shirts into a large suitcase telling herself she was an idiot for jumping whenever Parker held out a hoop. For falling into Parker's arms whenever he invited her in. Of course it was flattering to be needed. But what about her needs? She needed a family of her own. She just didn't know how to get one. And the longer she stayed connected with Parker and his family the longer she put it off, pretending, hoping, imagining he wouldn't care about a son to inherit the ranch. "Strictly business," he'd said. That's what she wanted and yet that's what she was afraid of.

When she arrived at the ranch that evening she was filled with anxiety. When she'd left she thought she'd never be back. As she slowly drove up the circular drive to the house she saw they were there on the front porch to greet her. Parker, Sarah, her grandfather, some of the boys. Her heart swelled with emotion and she blinked back the tears. The contrast between her cool, elegant town house and this solid, comfortable old ranch house struck her with the force of a boulder tumbling out of the mountains.

She barely got out of the car when Sarah came running down the steps to grab her and twirl her around. "I'm so glad to see you. I'm going to be so good from now on you won't even recognize me," she promised, with a meaningful glance at her father.

Christine laughed. How long had it been since she'd actually laughed? Did Parker know how fortunate he was to have a child to laugh with, to play games with, to ride with, read with.... He was still on the porch watching them with his shrewd blue eyes. How did he really feel about her coming there? Besides grateful, was he worried that she'd disrupt things, make another scene, criticize his parenting and then leave when the going got tough, like his wife did? Tempt him to forget why he didn't want to fall in love again? Probably not.

Christine walked slowly up the steps, while Sarah dove into her car to get her luggage. Christine said hello to the ranch hands, then bent over to inquire about Emilio's leg and inspect his cast. When she couldn't put it off any longer she said hello to Parker.

"I appreciate your coming on such short notice," he said. As if she were the plumber come to repair the leaky sink. His gaze was cool and steady. It was as if that interlude in the city had made a permanent rift between them. Either he was still angry with her or it didn't mean that much to him. But her heart was pounding like a jungle drum. She was surprised he couldn't hear it.

He'd changed back into a cowboy. Without the city clothes, his shoulders were broader, his legs longer, his face more suntanned, and the lines that gave his face character etched deeper than before. Had they really almost made love last night? And if they had, would he still greet her with the relief he'd feel if she were the vet come to save a sick sheep or the plumber to fix a leaky faucet? She reminded herself that she was the one who called it off. Who threw a wet blanket over their heated passion.

After Sarah lugged her two bags to the porch, Parker took them and led the way inside the house. "I've put you upstairs," he explained over his shoulder. "Pop's taking the den since he can't do stairs."

She nodded and followed him up the wide staircase. The men disbursed and Sarah and her grandfather stayed on the porch. Christine had never been upstairs, never knew whose bedroom was where. She found out. Parker turned right. The first bedroom was filled with medals and awards pinned to a bulletin board that almost covered one wall. On the bed was a pink-and-white flowered bedspread and in the middle of the floor Sarah's books and boxes and suitcases.

At the end of the hall was the bathroom, and flanking it two large bedrooms, one Parker's and one hers. "It was my mother's sewing room," he said, "and the guest room. I hope it's okay."

She looked at the fluffy white down quilt on the double bed, at the white lace curtains fluttering in the spring breeze and the old-fashioned bureau with a silver brush and comb on top. "It's lovely," she said simply.

He set her suitcases on the floor. Then he stood in the middle of the room and looked at her. The look in his eyes had the effect of shortening her breath and making her knees feel like putty. Oh, Lord, as much as she needed to be needed, she was never going to keep her cool while under the same roof as Parker. Especially on the same floor. She wrapped her arms around her waist. And braced herself for the speech about what he wanted and what he didn't want.

"Before you say anything," she said, holding up one hand, palm toward him, "I already know the rules ... unless they've changed in my absence."

He matched her palm with his and twined his fingers with hers. With eyes the color of the vast Colorado sky, he caught her gaze. "As a matter of fact, they have changed." He released her hand and gestured toward the bed. "Sit down."

She sank onto the firm mattress, into the folds of the soft quilt and stared at him, waiting.

Parker's gaze shifted to the open window and he cleared his throat. "I've been thinking about what you said," he said.

"I'm afraid I lost my temper," she said quickly. Why couldn't they just leave well enough alone? Forget their last encounter and pretend it didn't happen. She didn't have the stomach to rehash it now. He said it would be all business. That was fine with her.

"You were concerned about where our relationship was going," he began. "And I said this would be a business relationship," he continued, still staring out the window as if he hadn't seen the valley before.

She nodded vigorously. "And that's fine with me." It was, it really was, she assured herself. She knew one thing, she couldn't take any more ups and downs. No more hopes that would just be dashed.

"Is it?" he asked, suddenly turning his head and meeting her gaze. "I was hoping, wondering ... if you might give it a chance," he said. "*Us* a chance."

She blinked. She squeezed the folds of the down quilt in her fingers. "What?" she said stupidly.

"What you said last night shocked me. Made me angry. Furious. But you were right. I don't know anything about you." She opened her mouth to respond, but he shook his head. "You don't owe me an explanation. You don't owe me anything. Your debt to me is paid in full. But for some reason I can't leave it at that. As you said, I've been so caught up in what happened to me, I couldn't see what was happening to the people around me, you...Sarah."

Christine couldn't speak and wouldn't even if she could. She was held spellbound by the earnest look in his eyes, by the sincerity of his words.

"It's been a long time since my wife left. For the past twelve years people have been telling me to put it behind me. But I'm slow to catch on sometimes." He gave Christine a lopsided smile that made her heart turn over. "And then I never met anyone I thought I could care about, who was worth forgetting for...until you came along."

"Yes, but, Parker..."

"I don't know how you feel," he continued as if she hadn't interrupted, as if if he stopped now he'd never get it all out, "but I know there's something going on between us. Maybe it's just lust, maybe not. But I want to find out. I thought while you were here you might be willing to think about it."

"You mean think about how it would be..." As if she hadn't thought about it nonstop the whole time she'd spent at this place. How it would be if they were married, if this was their ranch, if Sarah were their child. The longing that filled her heart threatened to bring tears to her eyes. But this was no time for emotion. This was a time to keep a clear mind, a cool head, to be sure she understood.

"Yes," he said as if he'd read her mind. "How it would be if we lived here together. I won't say forever, because I realize after what I've been through..."

Christine nodded mutely. How could she say forever, either? What she should say was that she couldn't have children. Every man wanted a son to follow in his footsteps. Even a man who already had a daughter. And even if he got used to the idea of leaving the ranch to Sarah, he still wanted a son. He might deny it, but it had been ingrained in him forever by his father. A son to leave the ranch to. A son to inherit the land. And Christine could give him no son. No son or daughter. All she had to give was herself. And that wasn't enough. It wasn't enough for Michael and it wouldn't be enough for Parker, either.

But Christine didn't tell him. She told herself it was premature. He hadn't asked her to marry him. He might never ask her. He was only asking her to think about it. And while she was thinking, he might change his mind. He hadn't even said he loved her. He'd only mentioned lust. She ran her hands through her hair, perched on the edge of the bed, not certain whether she should jump for joy or burst into tears.

He walked to the bed and pulled her up to him, his hands on her arms. Two deep lines were carved between his dark eyebrows. "You haven't said yes," he said. "Are you angry that I brought you here under false pretenses?"

"You mean, Sarah doesn't need my help?"

He rested his broad hands on her hips and held her firmly in his grasp. "Oh, yes, she needs you. And I need you. We all need you. But do you need us?"

She nodded. Afraid to let him know just how much she needed, wanted, loved this place, this family, this man. The words were there waiting to be said. But not now. Maybe never. Not until he said them first. Not until she was sure of him.

Then he kissed her. A very different kind of kiss than the other ones, the frantic, explosive kisses they'd shared last night. This kiss started slow and gentle, a brush of his lips across hers, so tender it brought a sigh from deep down somewhere inside her. A sigh of longing, of hope reborn. Kiss followed kiss, as soft as the breezes that blew in from the window. As slow as the sheep that meandered across the meadow. As if they had all the time in the world.

Her hands crept around his neck, her fingers tangled in his thick hair and pulled him closer. She inhaled the scent of him, the leather and the grass and the sheer maleness that intoxicated her and made her want more. She wondered if she'd ever get enough of him. If they made love every night for one hundred years, would that be enough? She didn't think so. But she'd be willing to try. She reminded herself that for Parker this was just an experiment. That Parker was at a different place in this relationship than she was.

She broke the kiss and took a deep breath. "I suppose I ought to be getting to work. Cooking, I mean. After all, I am the cook here." It didn't hurt to remind him *and* herself that she was primarily there to cook and help Sarah.

He exhaled slowly, his eyes coming back into focus. He frowned and opened his mouth as if to protest, then he nodded. "Whatever you say."

Christine led the way downstairs. She gripped the banister hoping Parker wouldn't suspect just how much his kisses affected her, and how much she had riding on this "experiment." And how much she wished she could promise him a baby.

Sarah was standing at the foot of the stairs looking up at them. She was resting her chin on the railing as if she'd been waiting for them all this time. Christine pressed her lips together. She couldn't, she wouldn't, let Sarah get her hopes up about Parker and her.

"How'd you like your room?" Sarah asked.

"Wonderful. I love the view from up there."

"The location's good, too," Sarah said, her eyes brimming with fun.

Christine refused to play along. "Want to help me make dinner?" she asked, putting her arm around Sarah's narrow shoulders.

Sarah nodded with a glance at her father that said, "See? See how good I can be? How helpful?"

Christine smiled to herself and in the kitchen as they mixed up a batch of sourdough rolls for dinner Sarah told her why and how she was expelled. Christine talked it over with the girl, relieved to see that Sarah was subdued by the possible consequences of her misbehavior.

That night Parker came to the kitchen just as Christine was shaking freshly grated Parmesan cheese over the rigatoni before she carried the platter to the dining room. He stood in the doorway watching her before she noticed him. "I, uh, would you like... I mean, would you mind eating out there with us or..." He hesitated.

"With you?" she asked.

"Yeah. I mean we'd—*I'd* like it if you would."

"I guess I could." She studied him for a long moment, knowing it wasn't easy for him to ask, wouldn't be easy to have her sit with the men and his father and try to pretend she belonged there. But this was part of the plan, the "experiment" to see if she could fit in, to see if she could fit the role of ranch wife and mother. Mother. The word clogged her throat even though she hadn't said it. "Sure," she said with a quick smile. "Why not?"

He looked relieved, then helped her carry the food out to the bunkhouse. A hush fell over the dining room as she took the empty seat next to Sarah in the middle of the table. The men stole glances at her but didn't speak directly to her even once. As for Christine, she listened to their talk of sheep, sheep and more sheep and only picked at her food. And she couldn't help longing for the solitude of the kitchen where she could relax between courses, even peruse the cookbook or the evening newspaper while nibbling on her salad. But she'd promised Parker she'd give it a try. Give *them* a try, and she guessed this was part of it. Somehow they all got through the awkward dinner. Afterward Sarah helped her clear the table and load the dishwasher. Then before Parker could come by to see how she was doing, she said a hasty good-night to Sarah and tiptoed upstairs to her new room.

She didn't turn on the light though dusk was falling outside her window over the vast valley. She braced her hands on the windowsill and gazed out at the mountains in the distance, pondering the turn of events that had brought her back to the ranch. Wondering how long she'd stay this time. Wondering if anything in her life would ever be forever.

After breakfast the next morning Christine and Sarah went to the girl's room and did a survey of what she had to do to complete the school year. The math book overwhelmed Christine, but Sarah seemed to be good at the subject and wouldn't need much help. It didn't mean, however, that Sarah was prepared to spend the morning doing math or any other schoolwork. She gazed out the window with a dreamy look on her face when Christine was quizzing her on the causes of the Civil War.

"Sarah, did you hear me?" Christine inquired.

"Huh? Yeah, I heard you, but I was thinking about Sugar and how she needs her exercise."

"And so do you, I suppose," Christine said, narrowing her eyes. What had she done, promising to discipline this headstrong child when she knew absolutely nothing about children? "We *will* have recess, but first you have to answer the questions at the end of this chapter," she said sternly.

Sarah's eyes widened. Her gaze shifted from the outdoors to Christine. She bit her lip thoughtfully, then dutifully opened her book.

"And while you're reading, I'm going downstairs to check the soup I left on the stove."

With a brief backward glance over her shoulder, Christine left the room. She had a sudden recollection of her own mother helping her do her homework when she was home from boarding school. And so it goes, she thought, the circle of life, mothers helping daughters. Only Sarah wasn't her daughter. She didn't have a daughter, and would never have one of her own.

She seasoned the soup with salt and pepper and a dash of Worcestershire sauce, then went back to Sarah and they worked on vocabulary until noon when Sarah helped her make a salad to go with the soup.

After a short horseback ride together, Christine and Sarah returned to tackle irregular French verbs and dinner preparations. Another awkward dinner in the dining room set the pattern for the rest of the week. A week during which Christine took pains to avoid Parker. Because if she saw him, she'd have to talk to him, and she didn't know what to say. They were past the point of small talk. And yet not ready to talk seriously about themselves. And Christine was afraid if he touched her she wouldn't hesitate to fall into his arms and make love. And then what?

As she walked quietly down the stairs, barely conscious of the loud music blaring from the stereo in Sarah's room, Christine was so wrapped up in her thoughts she almost didn't see Parker standing at the foot of the stairs. He was only a shadow in the dark hallway. She sucked in a short, quick breath and tripped on the stair tread. He reached up to steady her and she stopped where she was, on the third step from the bottom, with his hand on her left arm. She'd so successfully avoided him this past week she didn't know what to say now that they were face to face with no one else around.

"Got a minute?" he asked.

She nodded mutely. She had a minute, a hour, even a lifetime, if that's what he wanted.

"Come out on the porch." He pulled her down the stairs toward him until standing on the bottom step she was on a level with him and could look straight into his deep-set eyes. What she saw was intense longing, desire and confusion, all mixed together. The same emotions she felt.

Parker put one hand on Christine's shoulder and they walked out the front door onto the porch. It was a warm evening, the cicadas filling the air with the sounds of summer. He pulled two lounge chairs together and they sat down. And stared up into the starry sky. He didn't know what he was going to say. He just knew they couldn't continue the way they were, with her keeping him at a frosty distance.

"Is there something bothering you?" he asked finally.

She turned to him. "Me?"

"I thought we had an agreement. We were going to give it a try. *Us* a try. Instead you've been avoiding me like the bovine flu. Shutting me out. What happened?" He planned to stay calm, but the frustration that had been building threatened to explode. He gripped the edge of the wooden armrests, wanting to hear, but afraid to find out she was only interested in being his cook or a friend to Sarah. His stomach twisted in pain when he realized she might very well tell him she just wasn't interested in him.

"Maybe all you feel toward me is gratitude," he suggested. Might as well make it easy for her.

"There is that," she agreed.

"Is that all?" he demanded. "If it is, I want to know now. Before I . . ."

"What?"

"Before I lose any more sleep over it."

She sighed deeply, her eyes downcast. "It's a long story."

He stretched his legs out in front of him. "I've got all night."

"It might take that long."

"Shoot."

She looked at him then and he was struck by the sadness lurking in her gray eyes. He wanted to take her hands in his, put his arms around her and tell her everything was going to be okay, but he sensed she didn't want any easy reassurances. So he pressed his balled-up fist into the palm of his other hand and forced himself to stay where he was.

She stared off into space, somewhere beyond the mountains on the other side of the valley for such a long time he was afraid she'd changed her mind and wasn't going to tell him anything except what he already knew. Instead she dragged her gaze back to his and began a painful excursion into her past, pulling him with her as she went.

Chapter Ten

"My parents were divorced when I was young—five or six, I guess." Christine said with a faraway look in her eyes. "Maybe that's why I feel such sympathy for Sarah. Not only that, but I was sent to boarding school just like she was and I hated it, too. But my mother was going through a difficult time and maybe my father was, too. I don't know about that. He hasn't really been a part of my life for many years. He remarried and had more children and well..." She trailed off and Parker found himself watching her, on the edge of his seat, waiting for her to continue.

"Anyway, I went from boarding school to college..."

"Where you learned to love poetry," he said, remembering her and Sarah bent over the poetry book.

She nodded. "And art and music. But nothing useful. No way to earn a living."

"Did you have to?" he asked, noting her hands lying still and calm in her lap. Beautiful hands, long and slim with tapered fingers. Hands that mixed and kneaded and chopped. Hands that could bring him to the brink of ecstasy. He raised his gaze to look her in the eye.

"No, I guess I didn't. My grandfather had left me some money in a trust. The same money I live off now. Maybe it would have been better if he hadn't. But that's beside the point. I arrived at college feeling like a refugee. Sent from place to place by my parents. Nobody wanted me, or so I thought.

"Which brings me to the present," she said with only a slight tremor in her voice. "Or close to it. Before I landed in your pasture, I was going to be married."

"To the diamond necklace," he said bitterly. He resented everything about the guy without knowing anything about him.

She gave a faint smile. "Yes. I almost made it to the altar in fact. I had the dress and even a whole slew of presents. But when I went in for my physical exam the doctor told me that I couldn't have children, couldn't sustain a pregnancy. I underwent every test that they could think of, but the diagnoses were the same." She said the words slowly, carefully, so there could be no mistaking them for something else. Either by him or her.

"What about in vitro fertilization or..."

She shook her head. "Not for me."

He frowned. "So you didn't get married. Why not?"

She leaned forward. "Why not?" she asked incredulously. "Nobody wants to marry a woman who can't bear children."

"I don't believe that," he said, feeling his blood pressure rise. "Who is this guy who wouldn't marry you just because you were infertile?"

"Michael Taylor Thomas the Fourth, who's expected to produce a Michael Thomas the Fifth. I don't blame him. He was under a lot of pressure from his family. I understood. I really did." She had her elbows on her knees now, looking so earnest it almost broke his heart.

"Well, I don't. If he wanted kids so badly why wouldn't he adopt?"

"Would you?"

"If I wanted them."

"But you don't."

"I have Sarah. She's all the children I need."

"Yes, I see. You're lucky, you know."

"I *didn't* know how lucky. Not until you came along." He took her hand in his.

But she pulled it away and braced her arms against the chair. "I didn't mean to unload all this on you." She looked around at the latticework that framed the porch, as if seeing it for the first time. "It must be the change of scene, or the hour or..."

"Maybe it's me," Parker suggested. "I'd like to think you wanted to confide in me."

"I owed you some kind of explanation," she said.

His blue gaze turned cool. "You don't owe me anything. Not the story of your life, not an explanation. Nothing. If that's why you're cooking for me and taking care of Sarah, then you can go. I don't want your thanks anymore, Christine."

She was surprised at the tension in his voice. "What do you want?" she asked. "You said you wanted me to give us a chance. But that was before you knew. Before you knew that I can't have children." She buried her face in her hands to hide her tears. The tears she could no longer control. When she finally stopped crying, she looked up at him with questions in her eyes.

"I still want to give us a chance," he said firmly. He waited. She didn't say anything. So he asked again. "So where do we go from here?" His voice was rough and deep in the silence.

"You said Sarah was all the children you wanted."

"Yes. As you can see, she's a handful."

"But if you *did* want more, you'd adopt?"

"I'm not sure," he said with a frown. "I've never really thought about it before. But is this about me, or you? Would you adopt a child?"

"I—I don't know. When I see how difficult it is to raise a child by yourself..."

"And what a mess I've made of it," he added ruefully.

She reached out to put her hand on his arm. "No you haven't. Not at all. Sarah's a wonderful girl. If I thought I could do half as well..." She trailed off. She noticed he didn't offer to go in with her on any adoption plan. Maybe if she had a twelve-year-old she wouldn't, either.

But she didn't. She didn't have a child and she didn't have a husband. And it didn't look like she was going to get either one. Especially if she hung around here waiting, hoping, praying that Parker would come around to wanting her enough to start a new life, a new family. She might as well realize that he meant what he said. He had one child and one was enough. Where did that leave her? On her own again. "You can go," he'd said. Yes, she would go, but not yet.

"Let's not go anywhere from here," she said, taking a deep breath to calm herself. "I'll stay until Sarah's all straightened out. Until her situation is stable and she doesn't need me anymore. Then I'll leave. Because after all, I have things I want..." She trailed off and glanced up at the screen door where a shadow flickered against the light from the living room. "Sarah?" she called.

Parker got to his feet and looked inside. "No one there," he said to Christine.

She stood. "I thought I saw...just for a minute. I hope to heaven she didn't hear us." She stood and opened the door to the living room. She tried to remember what they'd said, how it would have sounded if someone had overheard. But no one had, she told herself. She walked into the house with Parker at her heels. She had nothing more to say.

She felt drained and emotionally exhausted. Without a backward glance she murmured good-night and climbed the stairs. The music was still blaring from Sarah's room as she passed. Christine closed her bedroom door behind her, hoping Parker wouldn't knock. He didn't. He didn't even pause when he passed her room on his way to his. She breathed a sigh of relief. Relief mingled with sorrow too deep for any more tears.

Christine was exhausted. It was due to the tears and the frustrations of the day. But there was also relief. There were no more secrets between them. Parker understood her and she, unfortunately, understood him. She wanted a mate and child, he'd already had one of each. More than enough. She and Parker were attracted to each other, but it was a flame that burned too hot to last. It would burn itself out and then they'd part without tears or regrets. She fell asleep as soon as her head hit the pillow.

It seemed to be only minutes later that Parker was shaking her by the shoulder. "Christine, wake up. It's Sarah. She's gone."

She sat upright and snapped the night-light on. "What? Where?"

His face was pale, his eyes hollow sockets. "I went to tell her to turn the music off and I found this note addressed to you." He thrust it at Christine. *You guys are so dumb. You don't get it, do you? I'm leaving. You stay.*

Christine pressed her hands against her temples and swung her legs over the edge of the bed. "I *don't* get it," she said, grabbing a shirt and pulling it on over her nightgown. "What did I say? What did she hear?"

He shook his head while she yanked on a pair of sweatpants. "I don't know. All I know is her horse is gone. But she can't be very far. She's had—what, two hours?"

"Have you called around?"

"The two ranches adjoining ours. They haven't seen her. I'm sure she's not going to knock on somebody's door. She's hiding until we 'get it.'" They hurried down the stairs. Parker put his finger to his lips. "I don't want Pop to get wind of this. He'd worry."

"Right," she whispered. "She's probably in a barn or an outbuilding or something, don't you think?"

"Probably. So I'm going out on my horse."

"Can I come?"

He paused at the back door. "Sure, but you don't have to. She's not..."

Christine's lower lip trembled. "My daughter, I know, but I love her anyway and I feel like I'm to blame."

"That's ridiculous," he said shortly.

Christine followed him out to the barn, grateful that he couldn't see the angry flush on her cheeks. Did he mean it was ridiculous for her to love his daughter, or ridiculous for her to take any blame? Either way he was shutting her out. Refusing to let her be part of his life, part of his family.

Briskly he saddled both horses, his and the mare she'd ridden while she was there. They rode together out into the night without speaking. Christine didn't know where they were going and she didn't ask. He made her feel like she didn't have the right to know.

She tried to recall her exact words on the porch and how they could have been misinterpreted. But all she could remember was saying she'd stay until Sarah didn't need her anymore. It was so ambiguous as to be misinterpreted many ways. It could mean she'd stay until Sarah was eighteen, or until next week. If they found her—no, *when* they found her—she'd explain ... Yes, how would she explain when she didn't really know how long she'd stay?

She loved Parker, that much was clear. And maybe he loved her. But she wanted children, a baby to raise, to rock to sleep at night, to rejoice over its first step, first word, first day at school. She knew enough to know a single person had a slim chance at adopting a baby. Even if she could, and even with her financial resources, would she have the emotional strength to do it alone?

Maybe it was time to give up her dream, she thought as they galloped through the fields. Maybe it was time to move into the future. A future with Parker was worth pursuing, even if it meant giving up the idea of a child of her own. They'd have Sarah. As soon as they found her.

In her reverie and because of her slower horse, she'd fallen behind Parker. She called to him and he waited for her to catch up. "Where are we going?" she asked breathlessly.

"Toward the Livermores' spread. Sarah used to play there as a child. I don't know," Parker said, his vocal cords taut. "I don't know what else to do, where else to go." He held the reins with white-knuckled fingers. His mind was spinning like a top. She'd threatened to run away before, when he'd disciplined her, but she'd never done it. What had pushed her over the edge this time? If he were running away, he'd go to one of the weathered sheds that dotted the grassy landscape. But which one? She knew the area as well as he did. Maybe better.

He pulled up in front of an old abandoned sheepherder's cabin, jumped off his horse and threw the door open. The musty smell of old wool greeted him, but nothing and nobody else. He looked up and shook his head at Christine who waited patiently on her horse in the pale moonlight, her eyebrows drawn together, her lips pressed tightly together.

She did love Sarah, he thought. She worried about her, cared about her almost as much as he did. If she were Sarah's mother, she would never have left her. If she were his wife and Sarah's mother, they would have had more children, a whole houseful. But it was too late. Sarah was almost a teenager. And she'd need more supervision, not less. It wasn't fair to ask Christine to take her on. He motioned to Christine and they headed off to investigate other cabins, other barns, and never found a trace of her. The sun was rising over the mountains in the east when they rode toward the Hendersons' back forty acres just in case...

Adoption. He'd never thought of it before. Why should he? He had no reason to adopt. The Georges over in the next county had adopted a couple of Vietnamese orphans and they'd turned out all right. Turned into valedictorians and went on to college in fact. People said you loved them just like they were your own. No, that couldn't be. He'd never love another child the way he loved Sarah. However much trouble she gave him, she was his baby. Always would be. The twelve years had passed in a flash. He could remember the day they brought her home, holding her in his arms, inhaling her sweet baby smell...

Christine had never known that special feeling, of the tiny fingers wrapped around hers.... If she adopted a baby... if *they* adopted a baby.... If he could persuade her to marry him... If she knew how much he loved her. If she loved him. So many ifs. First they had to find Sarah. She was nowhere. She'd vanished in the vast Colorado grasslands.

At dawn he pulled up at the far northwest corner of his ranch, took his hat off and waited for Christine to catch up to him. "Let's go back," he said, noting her slumped shoulders. He had to get her home to get some rest. "See if there's any word. Maybe she came home," he said, but in his heart he knew she hadn't. He just didn't know where to look anymore. And he was worried about Christine. She wasn't used to riding this far and this hard. She didn't complain, but her cheeks looked hollow and her eyes red-rimmed.

She nodded, but he knew she didn't believe Sarah had returned, either. They trotted slowly across the field in the early morning dawn without speaking. Christine saw the shoe before he did. A size eight white athletic shoe that belonged to Sarah lying on the ground. Christine yelled, got off her horse and held it up triumphantly.

"What does it mean?" she gasped.

"Maybe she *is* home," he said, his heart pumping wildly.

"Go ahead," Christine said, with a wistful look at old Cindy, knowing she couldn't keep up with Parker.

With a burst of speed Parker raced across the grazing land toward the ranch house, leaving Christine behind to ride her tired horse as fast as she would go.

Sarah was leaning against the barn when he got there, barefooted, a smudge of dirt on her cheek, tears welling in her eyes as her father rode up. He slid off his horse and his knees shook so violently he was afraid he'd fall down. Then he grabbed her tightly in his arms.

"Sarah..." he began, half-furious, half-relieved. "Where were you?"

"In Mulholland's barn," she said in a quivery voice.

Mulholland. The one place he didn't look.

"I'm sorry," she said, her face buried against his chest. "I didn't mean to..."

"What did you mean to do?" he asked, frowning down at the top of her head.

"Get you guys together. Make Christine stay." She gulped loudly. "I heard what she said. She'd stay until I got straightened out. Well I'm not straightened out. I need help. I need you and I need her. And you need each other. You don't even know it, do you?" she asked, her eyes wide and bleary.

Parker shook his head with disbelief. Where did a twelve-year-old get these ideas? How did she get so smart so fast? "So you thought if you ran away we'd realize that you weren't okay, that you needed Christine to stick around. You've got some idea that she'd stay here if only she realized how much you need her."

Sarah nodded, then dropped her head to her chest. "But during the night when I was cold and hungry and thinking about it, I thought maybe I was wrong. Maybe I'd just scare her away cuz I'm so bad."

"You're not bad," he assured her, smoothing her hair. "Just a little mixed up."

"Did she already leave?" Sarah asked, raising her tear-stained face.

"No, of course not. She's been out looking for you, with me."

"She will leave though, won't she? And it's all my fault."

He held his daughter at arm's length and looked into her eyes. "Christine is here now because I asked her to come. Because you and I, we both needed her. And she agreed to stay until we don't need her anymore. But—"

"But that'll be never," Sarah interrupted.

"Yeah," Parker muttered. "I know."

He was filled with a sudden sadness knowing that there was nothing he could do to make Christine stay there. He could try throwing himself at her feet, promise her a whole orphanage if she wanted it, but if she didn't want him, if she didn't *love* him, she wouldn't stay. He turned as he heard hoofbeats in the distance. "Here she comes," he told Sarah.

Sarah bit her lip and threw her father a frightened look. But Christine was off her horse before the old mare had even come to a complete stop and she'd wrapped her arms around Sarah and hugged the girl so tightly Sarah couldn't have recited the apology she'd been practising if she'd wanted to.

Christine's tears of relief flowed freely and mingled with Sarah's. Between sobs Sarah managed to tell Christine how sorry she was and how she hoped she'd stay with them forever. Christine lifted her head and met Parker's gaze. "Forever's a long time," she said.

He nodded. "We were hoping, Sarah and I, that you'd at least give it some thought."

Her mouth fell open in surprise. "What, staying here?"

"I know, you've got your own life now."

"Your own mother and your own house," Sarah added solemnly. "But..." Sarah looked back and forth between the two of them, and with all of her twelve-year-old wisdom realized that the situation was now out of her hands. She yawned and wiped one dirty hand across her face. "I gotta go in now," she said.

They watched her go, then turned to look at each other. Christine didn't know if she was hallucinating after a night without sleep or if Parker had really asked her to think about staying there forever. She couldn't read the expression on his face that was lined with fatigue. And she couldn't very well ask him to repeat it. Maybe he'd changed his mind.

"Well," she said lightly, "all's well that ends well."

"I'd like to think it was a beginning and not an end."

"Parker," she blurted, gripping the fence post, "what is it you want to begin?"

"Everything. You, me, a new family. I know, I said Sarah was enough of a family, but I was thinking tonight, thinking as I was looking for her, scared to death

I'd lost her, of Sarah as a baby. It was hard raising her by myself, but I wouldn't trade it for anything. And if we did it together, all of us, you and me and Sarah and Pop, it ought to be a lot easier, and a lot more fun."

Her heart was pounding, her head was floating somewhere above her body looking down at this improbable scene. Was this Parker Robinson suggesting marriage and adopting children? She had to be sure. "Are you saying you would marry me and adopt a baby?" she asked incredulously.

"Not *a* baby, some babies. If you want them, I mean," he said, his face creased with anxiety.

"Well, yes, of course I want them."

"What about me?"

She rushed into his arms, and buried her face on his shoulder. "I've wanted you ever since you rescued me. You know what they say about the person who saves your life, don't you?"

"You belong to them?"

"And they belong to you."

"We belong to each other," Parker told her, and then he framed her face with his broad hands and kissed her slowly and deliberately as if they had all the time in the world. And they did.

Epilogue

Christine paced back and forth in front of the picture window in the living room of the ranch house. Huge, flat snowflakes were falling outside, coating the bare branches of the birch trees, but she didn't see them. Her eyes were on the horizon, watching for a car, waiting . . .

She heard the back door open and then slam shut, felt a brief gust of cold air and turned to see Parker shrug out of his sheepskin jacket and hang it on the coatrack in the hallway. She tried to smile, but her lips quivered uncontrollably.

"Hey," he said, gathering her gently in his arms. "Be patient. We've been waiting almost a year. You can wait another hour or two."

"A year? I've been waiting all my life."

He smiled indulgently, and turned her in the direction of the window. "Look at that weather. It's going to take longer than they thought."

"Do you think it's dangerous?" she asked, her forehead puckering in alarm.

"Not if they drive slowly, which they obviously are." She shivered despite the warmth of the blazing fire in the hearth and he held her by the shoulders and looked into her eyes. "Don't you have something to do to get ready?"

"Ready? I've been ready for eleven months. As soon as we filled out the forms I started working on the room." She'd painted, papered, carpeted and decorated the former guest room where she'd once stayed. The chest of drawers was full, the old rocker in the corner sanded and varnished.

"As I remember, you couldn't wait to get out of your wedding dress and into your old painting shirt."

"You didn't mind, did you?" she asked, clasping his hands in hers. "You don't think I married you just to get a baby, do you? Because I would have married you anyway. You are all I really need in this world. As much as I love children, I love you more." She looped her arms around his neck and pulled his face down to hers for a deep, solemn kiss.

Reluctantly Christine broke away and ran her hands down the broad planes of Parker's chest, reveling in the solid strength of him, both physical and emotional. Knowing she owed her happy present and her bright future to him. "I *should* do something. Something useful." Something to keep her mind off of the impending arrival and the weather.

"Bake something," he suggested.

"I did. It's in the oven."

"Read something."

"I can't concentrate."

He shook his head in mock despair. "Come out to the barn with me. Sarah's out there."

She shook her head. "What if they call? I might miss them. You go ahead. I'll stay here and pace in front of the window."

"Good girl." He patted her on the shoulder. "Somebody has to do it."

With a fond backward glance he grabbed his jacket and left her there, doing what she had to do. He was sincere when he said somebody had to do it. He was just as nervous as she was about the new arrival, but he couldn't show it. Not in front of her. If she weren't watching for the car, he'd be there glued to the window, gnawing on his fingernails.

The barn smelled of hay and animals grateful to be in out of the cold. Sarah was brushing her prize Angora goat until the pure white wool lay thick and straight. She looked up when her father came through the side door.

"She's looking good," Parker said, pulling up a milking stool and sitting next to his daughter.

"I thought you didn't like goats," she said, tilting her head in his direction.

"I didn't. Until I met Rocky here," he said, running his hand over her silky fleece.

"Her name is not Rocky. Her name is Blanche. Okay, so I thought she was a he at first. I had a lot to learn about goats."

"You and me both," her father confessed.

"What about babies?" she asked, holding a handful of grain under Blanche's nose. Her tone was casual, but he noticed an anxious look in her deep blue eyes.

"Well, let's see. As I remember, they're a lot like goats. At least, you were. And you're the only one I've ever had.'' He tousled her hair and she smiled to herself.

''How do you mean?''

''Well, Blanche here was born with lots of hair and so were you.''

''I was?''

''Yep, beautiful hair, just as soft as hers.'' He nodded at the goat.

''Goats can run and jump four hours after they're born,'' she noted with a sideways glance at her father.

''Oh, yeah? Well that's where they're different. You couldn't run or jump right away, but you could smile when you were six weeks old. And wrap your hand around my finger. And say Dada.''

Her eyes widened. ''Did I really?''

He nodded. ''You were the smartest and the cutest baby I ever saw.''

She turned her head, but not before he saw her blink back a tear. ''But was I good?''

''Good? You were the best baby there ever was. You never cried, except when you had good reason.''

''What about...''

''Baby Jane? She's got a lot to live up to, being your little sister. Christine's counting on you teaching her everything you know. About horses, sheep, goats, math, history, poetry...everything. This place is going to be yours one day, you know, yours and hers and whoever else comes along.''

''Does Pop know about that?''

''He's the one who suggested it.''

''But you always said...''

''I was always wrong. I didn't realize how much you loved this place and how much you belong here. Not till you came home. When I sent you away to school I thought it was the best place for you. But it wasn't. And I'm real sorry about that."

She shrugged off his apology. "Then Baby Jane can stay home. You won't send her away to school?"

"Not unless she wants to go. Everybody's different. Maybe she'll want to raise rabbits instead of goats. Maybe she'll want to play the violin instead of making goat cheese."

"She can play her violin while I'm milking my goats. They love music. It increases productivity," she said solemnly.

"You've got it all figured out," Parker said with a fond smile. Then he stood and cocked his ear. "Did you hear a car?"

Sarah gasped, tossed her brush to one side and together they ran back to the house through the softly falling snow.

Christine was holding the door open for them, her face pale except for the red spots on her cheekbones. Parker put one arm around her and the other around Sarah. Pop had heard the car and come hobbling from his room. All eyes were on the dark red sedan parked in the driveway and the woman who got out of the driver's side and came around to open the passenger door. Parker and Christine and Sarah melted together as one.

"What if they forgot her?" Sarah asked anxiously.

"What if she has no hair?" her father teased.

"What if she is a he?" Christine wondered.

Exchanging worried looks, they hurried down the stairs Christine had swept twice that day already.

"Sorry we're late," the first woman said.

"It's the weather," said the other, carefully holding a baby—*their* baby—in her arms.

Christine thought her lungs would burst, thought her legs would collapse, thought she'd faint dead away if they didn't *show* her, *give* her that baby now.

But the social services lady held on to the baby until they were all in the living room, seated on their couch. A hush fell over the room, broken only by a log crackling in the fireplace. Parker almost expected to hear a drum roll. The social worker unwrapped the baby and handed her to Christine.

They counted her toes, they examined her tiny ears, they oohed and aahed and pronounced her a perfect baby. She seemed to be equally pleased with them, bestowing her calm gaze on each in turn as if to say, "Yes, you'll do nicely. And by the way, when is dinner?"

Christine shifted the baby in her arms and reached for Parker's hand. "This is the happiest day of my life," she said.

"You said that on our wedding day," he reminded her.

"I didn't think it could get any better," she said, remembering that same living room full of guests, the flowers and her white satin dress. "But it did."

"I've got a feeling," Parker said, "that you're going to say the same thing next year."

"And the year after that," Sarah predicted, counting her baby sister's tiny toes once more. And she was right.

* * * * *

Silhouette's recipe for a sizzling summer:

* Take the best-looking cowboy in South Dakota
* Mix in a brilliant bachelor
* Add a sexy, mysterious sheikh
* Combine their stories into one collection and you've got one sensational super-hot read!

Summer Sizzlers

MEN OF *Summer*

Three short stories by these favorite authors:

Kathleen Eagle
Joan Hohl
Barbara Faith

Available this July wherever
Silhouette books are sold.

Silhouette®

TM

SS96

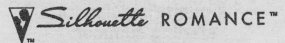

Silhouette ROMANCE™

is proud to present Carla Cassidy's
TWENTY-FIFTH book:

DADDY ON THE RUN
by
CARLA CASSIDY
(SR #1158, June)

Book four of her miniseries

Just when she was beginning to rebuild her life, Julianne Baker's
husband, Sam, was back! He had left only to protect her and their
little girl—but would Julianne be able to trust her husband's love
again, and give their family a second chance at happiness?

The Baker Brood: Four siblings in search of justice find love along
the way....

Don't miss the conclusion of **The Baker Brood** miniseries,
Daddy on the Run, available in June, only from

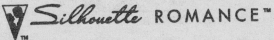

Silhouette ROMANCE™

BAKER4

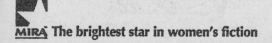

**The wedding celebration was so nice...
too bad the bride wasn't there!**

*Runaway
Brides*

Find out what happens when three brides have a
change of heart.

Three complete stories by some of your favorite
authors—all in one special collection!

YESTERDAY ONCE MORE
by Debbie Macomber

FULL CIRCLE
by Paula Detmer Riggs

THAT'S WHAT FRIENDS ARE FOR
by Annette Broadrick

Available this June wherever books are sold.

Look us up on-line at:http://www.romance.net

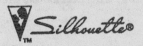

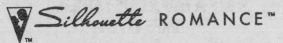
Silhouette ROMANCE™

is proud to present Elizabeth August's
TWENTY-FIFTH book—and the next installment
of her much-loved series:

Smytheshire, Massachusetts

This sleepy little town has some big secrets!

A HANDY MAN TO HAVE AROUND
by
ELIZABETH AUGUST
(SR#1157, June)

Gillian Hudson was determined to stay in Smytheshire, even
if it meant having Taggart Devereaux as her protector! But
this rugged loner never left her side, and Gillian suspected that
Taggart's "visions" weren't all about danger—but reflected her
own dreams of wedded bliss.

Don't miss A HANDY MAN TO HAVE AROUND
by Elizabeth August, available in June, only from

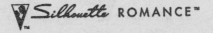
Silhouette ROMANCE™

This July, watch for the delivery of...

An exciting new miniseries that appears in a different Silhouette series each month. It's about love, marriage—and Daddy's unexpected need for a baby carriage!

Daddy Knows Last unites five of your favorite authors as they weave five connected stories about baby fever in New Hope, Texas.

- **THE BABY NOTION** by Dixie Browning
  (SD#1011, 7/96)

- **BABY IN A BASKET** by Helen R. Myers
  (SR#1169, 8/96)

- **MARRIED...WITH TWINS!**
  by Jennifer Mikels
  (SSE#1054, 9/96)

- **HOW TO HOOK A HUSBAND (AND A BABY)**
  by Carolyn Zane
  (YT#29, 10/96)

- **DISCOVERED: DADDY** by Marilyn Pappano
  (IM#746, 11/96)

Daddy Knows Last arrives in July...only from

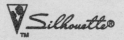

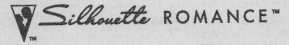